DUSK ALONG THE NIOBRARA

Dusk Along the Niobrara

John D. Nesbitt

FIVE STAR
A part of Gale, a Cengage Company

Farmington Hills, Mich • San Francisco • New York • Waterville, Maine
Meriden, Conn • Mason, Ohio • Chicago

LIBRARY OF CONGRESS CATALOGING-IN-PUBLICATION DATA

Names: Nesbitt, John D., author.
Title: Dusk along the Niobrara / John D. Nesbitt.
Description: First Edition. | Farmington Hills, Mich. : Five Star, a part of Gale, Cengage Learning, 2019.
Identifiers: LCCN 2018044044 (print) | LCCN 2018045917 (ebook) | ISBN 9781432858315 (ebook) | ISBN 9781432858308 (ebook) | ISBN 9781432858292 (hardcover)
Subjects: LCSH: Murder—Investigation—Fiction. | Ranchers—Fiction. | GSAFD: Western stories. | Mystery fiction.
Classification: LCC PS3564.E76 (ebook) | LCC PS3564.E76 D88 2019 (print) | DDC 813/.54—dc23
LC record available at https://lccn.loc.gov/2018044044

First Edition. First Printing: June 2019
Find us on Facebook—https://www.facebook.com/FiveStarCengage
Visit our website—http://www.gale.cengage.com/fivestar/
Contact Five Star Publishing at FiveStar@cengage.com

Printed in Mexico
1 2 3 4 5 6 7 23 22 21 20 19

For Cooper

But there is hope: you have yet to hear the shepherd.

—Choragos

CHAPTER ONE

The man named Dunbar came to the upper Niobrara country in the hottest part of summer, when the prairie grass had turned dry and thin. On a scorching afternoon when the air had grown heavy, I had come to a rest on a low ridge, hoping to catch a breeze for my horse and me, when a rider appeared out of the north. He was riding a light-colored horse and leading another that had dark markings and that at a distance appeared to be a packhorse. I waited as the man rode closer, but he and his horses did not grow very fast in my view.

By that point in my life—I was nineteen at the time—I already knew that the grasslands could deceive the eye. A distant point often turned out to be more distant than a person thought, and the land in between had more dips and swells than he would have expected. Cattle came into view on short notice, and antelope seemed to materialize out of the waves of grass. Objects also disappeared, as the oncoming rider did now.

I was left to ponder the landscape. The country beyond the point where I had seen him, bare and pale, stretched across in a low line of hills, east to west. I knew that beyond those hills, some ten miles or more, the Hat Creek Breaks rose higher, like a small range of mountains with pine trees and springs. But I could not see them. The intervening hills, formless in the haze and shimmering heat, blocked them from view.

When the traveler appeared again, closer, I could see that he was a tall man with a dark hat. He was riding a blue roan and leading a buckskin.

I waited for several minutes more. As the horses came within a hundred yards, I could hear them breathing. Their hooves thudded on the dry ground. Saddle leather squeaked. Tiny bits of dry grass rose with the dust from the horses' feet. Not wanting to stare at the man, I waited to let my gaze fall on him.

He wore a high-crowned hat that did not cast much of a shadow at the moment. He had dark hair, dark brows, dark eyes, and a bushy mustache. He wore a sand-colored canvas shirt with two chest pockets and a full row of buttons—not a common work shirt, but not out of place for a range rider. As he took a full breath, I saw that he had broad shoulders and a high chest. I guessed him to be in his middle thirties.

He brought the horses to a stop, touched his hat brim with a gloved hand, and said, "Good afternoon."

"The same to you," I said.

"Town of Brome is over that way, I imagine." He motioned with his hand in the direction behind me.

"That's right."

"Good to be up on a high spot and get my bearings." His voice had a friendly tone. "And those are the Rawhide Buttes, aren't they?" He motioned with his hat in the direction past my left shoulder.

I shifted in the saddle and saw the dark outline of Rawhide Mountain, some fifteen miles to the south and west, with the lesser buttes stretching north from it. "Yes, sir."

He took off his light leather gloves as he moved the blue roan close to me. He held out his hand and said, "My name's Dunbar."

"Pleased to meet you. My name's Bard Montgomery." We shook.

"Bard."

"Yes. It was my mother's family's name."

"Oh."

"It also means an old-fashioned poet. White-bearded type."

"I'm familiar with the term. A singer of heroic deeds and great tragedies."

I appreciated the cheerful spirit in his voice. "That's what I've understood," I said. I let my eyes drift over him. He had a rope tied to his saddle, in cowhand fashion, and he wore a dark-handled revolver.

"Lookin' for work," he said.

"Ranch work?"

"It's what I'm best at."

"There's not much else around here. Jobs in town get taken up pretty fast."

"That's all right. I don't shine much at weighin' out beans or deliverin' coal."

I took a broad view of the rangeland, treeless for miles in every direction. "I don't know if anyone's hiring right now. We're in between spring and fall roundup, of course."

"That's what I figured. It doesn't cost anything to ask, though."

I shrugged. "Not with me." I cast a glance over his packhorse. I like buckskins, and from what I could see of this one, he was a good-looking horse. I said, "I'm about ready to head back to the ranch where I work. If you want, you can ride along with me for a ways until I turn off."

"Don't mind if I do. What's the name of the outfit where you work?" He pulled on his gloves as he clucked to the horses and got them moving.

"Foster," I said, evening my reins as my horse began to walk. "Lou Foster. Has a small ranch in comparison to some, but he's good to work for."

"That's all you need. As far as work goes, anyway."

We rode on for a little ways with the only sounds coming

from horse hooves on dry ground, an occasional snuffle, and the creak of saddles. The heat bore down, and sweat poured out of me.

At length Dunbar said, "What do you think your boss would say about a fella stayin' over?"

"Happens often enough," I said.

"Always inclined to do a little work in return."

I tipped my head to try to shade out the sun where it had moved. "There's always work to be done."

Quietness settled in again, with only the sound of the horses as we made our way across the vast, open grassland.

Dunbar and I rode into the ranch yard from the west. The door of the bunkhouse opened, and Dan, the white-haired cook, stepped outside carrying a tin pail. He stopped at a young elm tree about six feet tall, and he poured the contents of the pail into the earthen bowl around the tree. Straightening up, he raised his free hand and waved to us. We waved back and rode on toward the ranch house.

I dismounted and called out, *"Yoodle-ooh!"*

The front door opened, and Lou hobbled out onto the small porch. He had a crutch under his right arm, as had been his habit for a few weeks. "What say?" he called out.

"We've got company, Lou, if it's all right. This is Mr. Dunbar, and he'd like to put up for the night." I turned and saw that Dunbar had dismounted.

Lou's eyes traveled over the stranger and his two horses. "Should be okeh. Passin' through or lookin' for work?"

"Work would suit me, if there is any." Dunbar took off his gloves and smiled.

"Well, put your horses up. We'll have grub in a little while."

"Thank you, sir."

"Your name again?"

"Dunbar."

"I like to be sure. I'm Lou Foster."

"A pleasure to meet you."

Lou made his way into the bunkhouse a little after we did. He hung his hat on a peg and shifted around on his crutch. Dunbar, his dark hair shining where his hat had been, stood up and stepped forward to shake the boss's hand. I stood up as well.

When they had shaken hands and Lou had rested his right armpit onto his crutch, he said, "Don't mind me. I'm not that crippled. I don't know what's wrong with this leg, but it hasn't been worth a damn for a while now. It's like a deep ache. I hope to get over it, but I can't count on it. Reminds me of an old horse I had, walked sideways in the hind end and dragged one foot. Came out of it a couple of times with better feed, but the last time, he didn't."

Dunbar smiled. "You're not that old."

"I'm fifty-one, for whatever that's worth. Not young, but not old. I hope."

Up until that moment, I did not know how old Lou was, but I would have guessed him at about fifty. He had creases on his weathered face, and gray was showing in his hair. He shaved about once a week, so he had stubble with a cast of gray as well. He had clear brown eyes, not filmy with age. He was not tall, and he was lean like a cattleman who had spent many long days in the saddle and had missed some meals.

Dunbar said, "Is the pain in the muscles or in a joint?"

"It's high on the leg here, right by the joint."

"I've heard of people having a cold settle into their joints, like a rheumatism."

"It wouldn't surprise me. I landed on this hip one time when I got thrown from a horse."

"I've also heard of people getting it from sleeping on the cold ground. I knew of one fellow who could barely walk at all, until he discovered he could walk backwards. That's how he got better. Took him a while."

"That sounds like me. I've gone backwards half my life."

Dunbar smiled. "Reminds me of a riddle," he said. "About the creature that goes on four feet in the morning, two feet in the middle of the day, and three feet in the evening." After a pause, he added, "Man, of course. Crawls on four feet in the morning, leans on a cane in the evening of his life."

"Well, I hope I'm not at that stage for good. Tapping the ground with a stick." Lou's eyebrows raised as if a thought passed through. "But sit down."

Lou sat in his chair at the end of the table, and Dunbar and I took our seats as before, opposite one another.

Dan came out of the kitchen carrying a steaming pot with both hands. For being an older man with dull white hair, pale blue eyes, and a pale complexion, he got around well enough, without any limps or hitches. He set the pot in the middle of the table.

"Beef stew. Hot biscuits comin' up."

We dug into our meal, and before long, Dan joined us. No one spoke, and the two tin plates of biscuits disappeared. When everyone had finished, Dunbar rose from his seat.

"If you show me to the dishpan, I can get started," he said.

Dan raised his pale blue eyes. "It's in the kitchen, but we wash the dishes at the other end of this table. More room."

"I'll fetch it."

When Dunbar returned with the enamel dishpan, he said, "This is a nice one. Good-sized, too."

Dan gave a single nod. "It doesn't go out with the wagon. I've got an old dented tin one that goes with the camp outfit."

"That's good."

"And we usually have two more fellas at the table, so you

14

picked a good time to volunteer. It's a good trick of George to take his turn when there's only two or three of us here. Bob, he finds it a good time to go to the little shack outside."

Dunbar glanced at the other end of the bunkhouse, where the cots were located. I imagined he had already counted how many had bedding. He did not seem to miss much.

He went to the kitchen and returned with the kettle that Dan used to heat water. Wisps of steam were rising from the surface.

"Use half for washing, and save half for rinsing," said Dan.

Dunbar nodded.

Lou rolled a cigarette and lit it. When Dunbar had his sleeves turned up and his hands in the water, the boss spoke.

"What kind of work are you looking for, Dunbar?"

"Right now, I'm employed at pearl-diving, but I do other kinds of ranch work as well."

"How are you at building corrals?"

"Planks or poles?"

"Planks. And square posts."

Dunbar rattled the silverware in the bottom of the pan. "Most cowhands I've met consider themselves pretty good carpenters. Which they may or may not be. But I know that building corrals entails a lot more than swingin' a hammer." He leveled his eyes at the boss. "Diggin' holes. Tampin' 'em in."

"Ha-ha. So you don't jump at it."

"Work's work. If that's what needs to be done, I'm willing to work at it. Do you plan to build them right here?"

I peered at the boss. This was the first I had heard of building any more corrals.

"No." Lou puffed out a small cloud of smoke. "It's a set of shipping pens. In town. By the railroad."

"I've got the idea."

"We'd like to have 'em ready for when we finish fall roundup, which means we have to have 'em done before we go out with the wagon. Each outfit is supposed to contribute some men. I'd be one of the workers, but for my leg. I thought I was going to have to split up Bob and George, or send this fellow who works for me part of the time, but maybe I could send you and Bard and Dan. What do you think? Your hands aren't gettin' too soft washing dishes, are they?"

"Not yet. I haven't been doing it every day. When does the corral job start?"

"As soon as the lumber arrives. I can keep you busy in the meanwhile."

"You can count me in."

The boss was reaching to tip his ash in a sardine can when galloping hoofbeats made him flinch. He flicked his hand, and the ash landed in the can. He frowned and said, "Who's that?"

The drumming of hooves stopped, and the bunkhouse door burst open. Bob Crenshaw and George Olney charged in.

The boss was still frowning. "What's wrong? You boys were supposed to sleep out and swing back tomorrow."

George spoke. "I know. But Bill Pearson's been killed. Shot."

The boss sat straight up. "The hell. When?"

"Earlier today, it looks like."

"Where?"

"On his own land, over by those chalky buttes."

I placed the area in my mind—northeast of the Foster ranch a few miles, where the land began to break up before it crossed into Nebraska.

The boss nodded. "Did you find him?"

Bob answered. "No. His wife did. She's all tore up about it."

"I'm sure she would be." The boss spoke to Dunbar. "That's the fellow I mentioned. Works for me from time to time." He returned to Bob and George. "I'll send someone over there tomorrow. You boys might as well stay here tonight. Put your horses away and get somethin' to eat. Don't waste time or you'll have to wash your dishes yourself. By the way, this is Dunbar."

Bob and George nodded and walked out, their bootheels thumping and their spurs jingling.

"This is no good," said the boss, taking up his cigarette again. "A poor man, barely makin' it to begin with. And now this. I pity his poor wife."

Dunbar and I set out the next morning for Bill Pearson's homestead. The sun had been shining red in the haze when I first went outside at sunrise, but it had climbed and turned pale by the time we left the ranch. Our route took us northeast across the grassland, again with no tree in sight. On a larger scale, this part of the country slopes downward as it stretches east from the Rocky Mountains to the flatter prairies of Kansas, Nebraska, and Iowa, but on our ride that morning, we made a gradual climb toward the chalky buttes and broken plains. Beneath the hazy sky, I had a sense of being on the eastern edge of Wyoming north of the Niobrara. I also had an awareness of carrying, in my inside vest pocket, an envelope containing gold coins that accounted for the last of Bill Pearson's wages.

I had dropped by the homestead a couple of times before, so I knew where it was. The shanty looked the same as always as it came into view—weathered lumber on the sides, and rough wood shingles on the pyramid roof. The front door was open, and darkness showed inside. Half a dozen molting white chickens pecked in the bare yard. We slowed our horses as we approached the house.

A feeling of dread ran through my upper body. I knew who Mrs. Pearson was, that her name was Georgiana, and that she and her husband had raised five kids who had gone their separate ways. But I did not know the experience of going to a dead man's house and trying to comfort his widow.

We drew rein a few yards from the house. Dust rose up

around our horses' knees as we dismounted. I felt a tightness in my throat.

The woman appeared in the dark doorway.

"Mrs. Pearson," I said. "I'm Bard Montgomery. I work for Lou Foster. He sent us over to help. He can't ride." I ran out of words, so I waited.

"I don't know what you can do. They took Bill to town."

"Bill had some wages coming. The boss sent 'em with me."

Dunbar spoke. "And the cook sent a loaf of bread, along with some cooked beef."

"You might as well come in for a minute. Get out of the sun."

The day was heating up. We tied our horses at the rail and followed her inside. Sweat trickled down my forehead as I took off my hat. Dunbar had removed his as well. The dark interior of the house had a strange and empty feeling to it.

I drew the envelope out of my vest and handed it to Mrs. Pearson. "Here's his earnings," I said.

She held the packet with both hands and stared at it. "Thanks." She raised her head, and I met her worried brown eyes.

"I'm sorry, ma'am. I don't know what else to say."

She shook her head, and her eyes watered. "Nothin' anyone can say will change anything. But I appreciate you coming here." She motioned with her hand at two wooden chairs. "Sit down for a few minutes. I know it's a long ride."

Dunbar handed her the two packages that Dan had wrapped in brown paper and tied with string. "Here's this."

"Thank you." She disappeared into the kitchen with the packages of meat and bread.

We took our seats. The chair that I touched felt sticky, but I wiped my hand on my trouser leg and thought no more about it. By now my eyes had adjusted, so I looked around the front room. A tattered bed cover was draped over the couch, with a pile of laundry on top that looked as if it had been taken off the line a few days earlier. Grime lay on the cupboard top and on the drawer handles. A tin coal bucket held twigs and splinters for starting a fire.

I returned to the moment as Mrs. Pearson came out of the kitchen carrying a wooden chair like the ones we sat on. I nodded and gave her my attention as she took a seat and put her hands together in her lap. Her face was harried, as could be expected, and her gray hair was not well combed. She wore a sagging dress that looked as if it had not been washed in a while, and she had spots and wrinkles on the backs of her hands.

Dunbar spoke. "I didn't know your husband, Mrs. Pearson, but I'm sorry for what happened to him. If there's anything I could do, I would be willing to help."

Her yellow teeth showed as she said, "I don't know what it would be."

"I don't, either. But if there's anything you could tell us, it might do some good."

Her eyes tightened. "Are you some kind of a lawman?"

He shook his head. "No, but I don't like to see people get away with something like this, and if there's anything I can do, I will."

She let out a tired breath. "Sometimes I wonder if anyone will do anything. I haven't gotten a sense that anyone in town really cares. The men that came for Bill, they acted the same way people did when the old horse trader was found dead. Seems as if they don't want to do or say anything that'll bring something upon themselves. I'll say this. If it was someone better off, someone important, then people would be doing things. Asking questions. Wanting answers. But when you're dirt poor, no one cares."

"Almost no one. But I do. And I think my young friend does."

Mrs. Pearson turned her eyes toward me, and I nodded.

Dunbar's voice had a considerate tone. "I don't know how much I can do, but I can try. And I've got to be careful myself. You can help if you can answer a couple of questions."

She gazed at him without much expression.

He went on. "I imagine you'll be asked this more than once, if you haven't been asked already. But do you know of anyone who might have had a reason to do this to your husband?"

She stared at the floor as she took a moment to answer. "I don't know if it would do any good to say. Or worse, if it would lead to harm."

"Not with us, I assure you. If you know of someone who might have had a hand in this, you'll be helping him, or them, by not saying anything."

She raised her eyes in a slow motion. "You say 'know of.' Maybe I do."

Dunbar's eyebrows went up. "Ah."

Before he could say anything else, she spoke again. "Bill didn't say much, and I don't know how much to repeat."

"Believe me, Mrs. Pearson. None of this goes beyond the present company."

She turned her head to take in each of us, and I gave what I hoped was an assuring nod.

"As soon as Bill's buried, I'm leaving. The kids can come and sell the property. I've got a sister in North Platte and another in Red Cloud. I won't say which one I'm going to."

"I don't blame you. But I promise you I won't repeat anything unless someone is brought to account. Nor will my young friend."

I nodded as before.

She heaved another tired breath. "Well, it might help. But like I say, Bill didn't tell me much. He thought there were some things I was better off not knowing too much about."

"Maybe he was right—" Dunbar left his comment hanging.

"And maybe he wasn't. I see what you mean." Her chest rose and fell. "Anyway, it goes like this. He said he saw a man recently that he had seen before, and he was afraid he let the man know he recognized him. The man gave him more than a dirty look."

"Did he mention the man's name?"

"No."

"And what did he recognize him from?"

"Bill said that he saw this man, back at about the time the old horse trader was killed, and this man was coming from the direction of the horse trader's place. It was winter, and Bill was out trapping and hunting."

"And he didn't say the man's name? Did he know it?"

"I believe he did, but he wouldn't say it. I think he thought that if I knew it, I could get hurt."

Dunbar smoothed his mustache with his hand. "How about someone else? Was there anyone who had a grudge against your husband or that he owed money to?"

"I don't know of any grudges, but he owed a bit of money here and there. Never anything very great. Maybe a little at the general store, some at the mercantile, maybe at the blacksmith's, and maybe a little at The Bower."

"What's that?"

"A small saloon in town."

Dunbar cast his eyes at me.

I shrugged and said, "I know where it is. That's all."

Dunbar spoke to Mrs. Pearson. "Anything else you can think of?"

She shook her head.

Silence held in the room for a few seconds until Mrs. Pearson said, "Would either of you like a cup of coffee? I could fix some."

"None for me, thank you," said Dunbar.

"No, thanks," I added. To Dunbar I said, "I suppose we should be going."

"I think so." He rotated his hat in his hands. "Is there anything we can do before we leave, Mrs. Pearson?"

"I can't think of anything. I've asked for a buggy from town. As soon as Bill is buried, you won't see me here again."

Out on the trail, I was glad to be riding under the big sky, even if the air was becoming heavy with the day's heat. I said to Dunbar, "I agree with you about not liking to see someone get away with something like this. And I agree with her. These people had very little to begin with, and now this poor woman has nothing, and she wonders whether anyone will do anything."

"That's just it," said Dunbar. "People kill for bad reasons, and it becomes worse when they think they can get away with it because the lesser people don't matter. It's not right." He pushed out his mustache and said, "I guess that last part is an obvious thing to say. But it doesn't make it any less true."

CHAPTER TWO

Cigarette smoke hung in the bunkhouse after breakfast. Bob, George, and Lou had all rolled pills, as George called them. Dunbar kept to himself with his chair pushed back as he drank coffee. I had gotten some tiny prickly-pear needles in my finger the day before, and I was straining my eyes trying to pluck them out. Dan, with his white hair and white apron, was moving around the table, pouring coffee.

The boss rested his cigarette on the sardine can. "Kid," he said, which was what he called me half the time, "you and Dunbar can ride together again today. I need to send a message up to Bancroft's. Dunbar can get the layout of some of the country. If you see any of our cattle too far north, push 'em back this way."

Dan said, "I think it's a good idea you're sending someone with him. He might forget to come back."

The boss smiled. "You wouldn't do something like that, would you?"

I said, "Not at all."

"Good." He looked past me. "Dunbar, you know which horses to pick from, don't you?"

"Yes, I do. The boys showed me yesterday. If you don't mind, I like to use mine once in a while as well, to keep them in shape."

The boss took a puff from his cigarette. "I suppose that would be all right. Hired men usually ride company horses, but I don't see anything wrong with it."

23

"Thanks. I'll let them rest another day or so, anyway."

"I'll leave it to you. Each man looks after his own string, you know."

"Sure."

"Bob and George, you ride west. Your usual pattern. Just don't get lost."

Bob smiled as he dipped his head. "We won't."

I picked out a bay to ride for the day. It was his turn. Not all the horses in my string let me walk up to them, but he did. Dunbar roped out a stocky brown horse, and we led our mounts to the barn together.

"That's Grumpy," I said.

"Thanks for telling me."

"It's just his name. He's a pretty well-behaved horse."

"So was the one I rode yesterday." After a moment of silence, he said, "Where do Bob and George get lost?"

"Ashton. It's the next town over on the railroad line. It's a bigger town. Crossroads. It's got a handful of saloons, a couple of fancy houses, card games, and I don't know what-all."

"I know the place. Not all the establishments, of course."

I shrugged.

"For example, there's a place that sells sewing notions. Never been in it. I buy all my needles and thread in Great Falls, Montana."

"I keep a good supply, too," I said. At least he didn't ask me about Dan's joke. Still, I was used to men joshing me.

The morning was dry and warm as we set out across country toward the northwest. From time to time we came to a rest on a high point to survey the surrounding country. The day promised to be hot, with the sun bearing down on us, but the meadowlarks were singing, and what cattle we saw were feeding on good grass.

As I was the one setting the course, I thought I would take us past Blue Wolf Spring. Such were the folds and rolls of the grassland that a person wouldn't know the place existed unless he rode within a half-mile from the south or the west. As I brought us near, the low clay bluffs and narrow canyon came into view. A few chokecherry trees, about ten to twelve feet tall, grew at the mouth of the canyon. The bottoms of the trees were trimmed level, as was common in cow country.

I brought us to a stop on the bare ground in front of the canyon. Cattle tracks and cow pies lay all around, and along one bluff, a scattering of bleached bones caught the sunlight.

"This is Blue Wolf Spring," I said.

Dunbar nodded.

"This is where the old horse trader lived, the one Mrs. Pearson referred to. His name was Alex Garrison." I pointed to a rectangle of rocks embedded in the ground. "I think that's where he had his cabin."

Dunbar nodded again, but he did not show great interest.

"He was killed, you know."

"That's what I understood."

I pointed at the wooden trough that was wet with spillage. "Over there is the spring where he watered his horses."

"I can see that. It brings cattle here."

"We can water these horses if we like," I said.

"Not a bad idea."

We dismounted and led our mounts to the trough. We loosened the cinches, and as the animals drank, Dunbar gave the area around us what I thought was a critical observation.

"You're not superstitious, are you?" I asked.

"Oh, no. Just thinking. This wouldn't be a bad place for a

picnic if it weren't for all the flies. Maybe on a sunny day in winter, up against the bluffs. No flies then."

We arrived at Bancroft's in the latter part of the morning. We had made a gentle climb for the last hour across the grassland, and as we came out on a level area, I felt a faint breeze from the west. At the same time, perspiration trickled down my back.

To the southwest lay Rawhide Mountain, at a greater distance than it had been a couple of days earlier when Dunbar had pointed it out. As before, it loomed as a dark shape, and I knew it was covered with pine and cedar trees. To the north, the Hat Creek Breaks rose from the plains. The southernmost reaches of the breaks lay a mile or two to the north of where we were, and I could see pine trees, dark specks against the tones of earth and dry grass.

As we rode up to the Bancroft place, I noted, as I had on earlier visits, that there were no trees. The yard was clean, and the buildings were painted—the barn was red, and the house was white. Horses stood in the corral swishing flies, and a tan nanny goat wandered free in the yard, doing her job of keeping the weeds down.

At our approach, the goat raised her head, opened her pink mouth, and called, *"Beh-heh-heh-heh-heh."*

Dunbar answered her with a similar sound.

Silence returned. I thought I had heard a banging noise in the barn when we were riding in, but it had ceased. About forty yards away, the barn door was open. I was about to call out when a bearded man appeared in the doorway. I recognized him as Del Bancroft, so I waved. He did the same and walked toward us.

In addition to his beard, he had a full head of brown hair. He was not wearing a hat, which I attributed to whatever work he had been doing in the barn. He was of average height and square build. He waved the goat aside as he walked past her, and his voice carried as he smiled at me.

"Hello, Tag." I think it was his way of calling me "kid" but softening it. "What are you up to?"

"Good morning. I think it's morning still." I squinted at the sky and came back to him. "I brought a message from Lou. By the way, this is Mr. Dunbar. He just came to work for us, and he'll be working on the corrals in town." I handed over the folded letter.

Del broke the wax seal, which I think Lou had applied as a matter of form and courtesy. Del nodded as he read the letter, then folded it and put it in his back pocket.

"Sounds like work," he said. "It's good for young fellas like you."

I smiled in return. "How's everything?"

"Oh, just fine. Except the coyotes put up quite a wail last night. Wouldn't let us sleep." He turned to Dunbar. "Are you a varmint hunter?"

"Not by trade. As you might guess, I'm a cowhand. Lately I've gained fame as a dishwasher at the Foster ranch, and they say they're going to make a post-hole digger out of me."

"Looks as if there'll be plenty of holes to dig. The ones that have rocks in 'em we'll give to young Montgomery."

"Are you a blacksmith?"

Del turned his smudgy hands palms up as he regarded them. "Not by trade. But I have a project I work on when I can find a few minutes. I'm restoring an old stagecoach."

"Sounds interesting," said Dunbar. "I never get tired of looking at old coaches and wagons and the like. Traces and harness."

Del motioned with his hand. "Come and take a look at it. You've got time, haven't you?"

Dunbar turned to me and raised his eyebrows.

"Sure," I said. "I've seen it, so I can water the horses. Go ahead." As the two of them walked away, I led the horses to the water trough that stood halfway between the house and the barn.

I loosened the cinches and let the two horses drink. I did not want them to drink a large amount all at once, so I pulled them back after they had drunk for a minute or so.

I glanced toward the house, but I saw nothing new. I led the horses away from the trough and kept myself from staring at the house. All in an instant, the door opened, and movement caught my eye. My pulse jumped. A light blue dress and brown hair shining in the sun told me it was Emma.

I caught a flash of her teeth as she smiled and waved.

I waved back, then took off my hat as I stood waiting with the horses at my side.

"Hello, stranger," she said. "Long time."

"I got here as soon as I could." I blinked at the sun. "Good morning."

A smile played on her face. "What brings you here?"

"Message from my boss to your father. Another rider, fellow by the name of Dunbar, came with me. Your father is showing him the stagecoach." I allowed my eyes to rove over her. My knees almost weakened at the sight of her dark eyes and her brown hair, the latter lying in a single braid over her shoulder in front of her, some strands lightened by the sun and twisted into variegation with the darker hair underneath. She had a slender face and a beautiful mouth. I had known her for more than three years, but I had not yet kissed her. I would have given just about anything to do so, and in my fancy, I recalled stories of Indian lads who would bring a string of ponies to a girl's father. In reality I did not expect to have to give anything, but I felt that I still had to wait. I thought I would know when the time came, and I hoped it would.

"What's new?" Her pretty teeth showed in contrast with her tan complexion.

"Not much. It looks as if we're going to be working on a corral project. The shipping pens in town."

She drew her brows in a thoughtful expression. "Oh, yes. I heard something about that a while back." After a pause, she said, "We also heard there was some trouble not far from you."

"Oh. I'd forgotten about it for a moment. Yes, there was."

"It's too bad. I understand he was very poor and had very little to leave his wife."

"It's sad, all right. Dunbar and I rode over there. The woman was very . . . distraught. Not just because she was poor, which she is, but because people don't seem to care enough to do anything about what happened."

Emma's brows drew together again. "But someone will look into it, won't they?"

"Oh, yes. It's been reported to the sheriff's office. But you know what people say. If it was someone a little higher up in status, people might be quicker to pay attention and do something about it."

"Do something about it. Isn't that the way people talk? It's so vague."

"Well, yes, it is." I decided she was not criticizing me in particular. "Mrs. Pearson says it's the same as what happened with the old horse trader. We passed by his place on the way over here."

"Old Alex Garrison. I've heard that story. My father was around at the time. And you're right—or she is. Not much was done."

"Well, I certainly feel sorry for her."

"So do I. To be poor and to be widowed, and to think that nobody cares. I don't know her, but my heart goes out to her." Emma drew her lips together, then spoke again. "We think that these things happen to other people—people who aren't like us. But the truth is, or my thought is, that if someone can do something like this to one group or set of people, they can do it to another." She moved back half a step and blinked her eyes. The sun shone on her brown hair and light blue dress. "I'm sorry," she said. "It's as if I came back to worrying about myself, or my family, after all."

"You've got good reason. You make sense."

"What should be important right now is helping her and trying to do something about this terrible thing. You see? I said it myself. Do something about it."

"She said she's going to go stay with a sister. So she has a plan that doesn't call for anyone's help from here. As for doing something about what happened to her husband, I don't know what you or I could do."

"Conscience itself is better than nothing. At least in our conscience, we don't go along with it."

"No, we don't."

Silence hung for a few seconds until she said, "On the lighter side, we might go to Lincoln."

My heart sank. "That's nice. When might you go?"

"Not until the fall. After the steers are shipped."

"Oh, well, that's a ways off." I was trying to think of how I could see her more often in the meanwhile.

"Yes, but it's the only thing that's new with us."

Being brought back to the moment, I was afraid her father and Dunbar would appear at any time. I said, "I don't know when I'll be able to see you again."

She smiled. "When you get a chance."

"What if I brought you something?"

"Depends on what it is. Don't bring me a toad, or a baby rabbit that's going to die in captivity. What are you thinking of?"

"Nothing in particular right now. Just the idea."

"That's fine. Oh, here they come."

As I was holding the reins of the horses with my right hand, I held out my left, palm upward. She reached forward with her right and pressed four fingers against mine. Our eyes met, and she had a perfect, sweet smile with the sun falling in a soft glow on her brown hair and sky-blue dress.

"Goodbye," she said. "I'll see you when you come again."

"Yes, I'll see you again soon. And goodbye to you." I did not let myself watch her retreating figure for more than a couple of seconds. I turned to see her father and Dunbar on their way from the barn.

"Ready to go?" called Dunbar when they were a few yards away.

"I believe so." I gave the reins a shake and separated them.

Dunbar drew to a stop, and before taking the reins, he turned to Del Bancroft and held out his hand. "It's been good to meet you."

"Likewise." The two of them shook.

Del reached forward and shook my hand. "Good to see you as well." Stepping back, he took in both of us and said, "Come again when you can stay longer."

"We sure will," said Dunbar.

"You bet," I added.

I handed Dunbar the reins to the brown horse. We led our horses apart and tightened our cinches. As we mounted up, I noticed that Dunbar pulled himself aboard with only one hand on the saddle horn. I imagined he was used to keeping his right hand free for the lead rope of his packhorse. Still, I thought he had to be very sure of a horse he was riding for the first time.

I turned the bay horse around, touched my hat brim in farewell to Emma's father, swept a glance at the house, and rode out of the yard.

Dunbar rode up alongside me. "Day's still young," he said.

"We would have had to contrive a long conversation in order to be invited to stay for noon dinner." When I didn't have an answer, he said, "It's just as well. We should have time for whatever work Lou has in mind for us this afternoon."

"I believe so." The thought came to me that I could have let the horses have another drink before we left, but I knew where there was a windmill if we took a straight line back to the ranch. I felt self-conscious, knowing that my nervousness at being seen with Emma had allowed me to forget to water the horses a second time. Then I had a good thought. I appreciated Dunbar not saying anything about her.

The gentle decline lay behind us, and the sun was nearing its high point of the day. The air did not stir. I was keeping an eye out for the windmill and beginning to feel guilty about the horses. I had to lift my hat every few minutes and wipe the sweat from my brow. Dunbar did the same, but he was not one of those fellows who turned red in the face and complained about the weather. To the contrary, he had a cheerful air about him.

We rode along without speaking. I fell into my own thoughts and was wondering what kind of a trifle I could buy or find for Emma when Dunbar spoke up. To me, his comment came from out of nowhere.

"Seems like a long way off in time, but this place gets covered with ice and snow in the winter, doesn't it?"

"Yes, it does. The drifts pack hard, and sometimes it's next to impossible to travel across them. Your feet or your horse's hooves break through and sink in to the knees or deeper. Legs get chafed. Each step is a chore. Cattle get stranded. People do, too."

"Then it all melts off, and you find the dead cattle, or even dead buffalo in some places, that died in the winter." He made a clucking sound.

"Seems like a long ways away, that's for sure."

"Time, of course. Not distance. But there are places, far from here, where it never melts."

"The frozen North."

"That's right. The northern part of Canada, on across Iceland and Greenland, northern Europe, and Russia. And farther south as well, places like the Alps, or even the Rockies. Snowfields, avalanches, glaciers. Now that's where people and animals really get stranded. Your field scientists excavate some of those places, and they've found mastodons and hairy mammoths that could be thousands of years old. Well-preserved." He pursed his lips in a droll way. "People, too. Frozen for centuries." His chest went up and down as he took a leisurely breath. "Then there's the more recent ones, recent being relative, but something that someone has a record of. For example, a man falls into a crevasse and is trapped in a glacier."

"Must be a terrible way to die," I said.

"Oh, yes. They say that freezing to death, in itself, is not so bad. Like a dream. But the panic and terror in the meanwhile— well, it has to be terrible, as you say. But once he's frozen, there he is, preserved. Sometimes the body comes out in the moraine—that's the rubble left behind—maybe seventy-five or a hundred years later. Another generation finds 'em. People who lose friends and family that way know they'll never see the person again, but there he is, all that time."

"It's too bad."

"Yes, it is. People who die like that most often have an idea of what they're doing—mountaineers, expeditionists, packers, traders. But they make a mistake, or they have bad luck. If things had happened differently, they could have lived longer, but at least it wasn't caused by someone else."

I thought I saw what he was getting around to, even if he

hadn't begun with that intention. "I see what you mean."

"Not like the late Bill Pearson, or the old horse trader Garrison, years ago."

He made such easy reference to Alex Garrison that I thought he must have taken more interest than it seemed earlier. I said, "I sure agree with you, along with what you said the other day about people thinking they can get away with things like that just because their victims are lower class." As soon as I said those words, I felt as if I had sounded crass. I added, "That is, lower from the perspective of the person taking the liberty."

"Well, not everybody is equal in terms of their station in life. That's evident. And some of the generalities people form are based in real life, like the idea that a poor man has a poor way of doing things. But still, this is supposed to be a country of opportunity where everyone is created equal and deserves an equal chance. That's why people come west. People like Bill Pearson or Del Bancroft. They believe in an equal chance. So do you and I."

"Of course I do."

"Sorry. I almost got stirred up there. I drifted away from those easy thoughts about people going off in a pleasant dream when they freeze to death."

"That's all right. It bothers me, too. Not to mention that if they get away with it in one instance, they might think they could do it again." I felt I should give Emma credit for part of my idea, but I preferred not to mention her at the moment.

"Oh, yes," said Dunbar. "If it hasn't happened already." I must have given an expression of surprise, for he added, "I meant the possible connection between Bill Pearson and the horse trader. Two things in the past. I'm not the kind who sees a mirage in the clouds and knows what's on the trail ahead."

We made it to the ranch in good time, having spent but a few minutes at the windmill. When I checked with the bunkhouse clock, I saw that the round trip took about five hours. Not only did we arrive on time for the noon meal, but we were ahead of the other three men.

Dan was setting plates on the table as we took our seats. "What's the news from up north?"

"Greenland?" I asked.

"You know what I mean."

"Of course I do. And I can't remember anything new." I tossed a glance at Dunbar.

"We stopped off at Blue Wolf Spring on the way up," he said.

"Uh-huh." Dan did not look up.

"Bard told me a little about the old horse trader who used to live there."

Dan took spoons out of his apron pocket and placed them upright in the crockery jar. "Garrison. His name was Alex Garrison."

"That's what he said. I guess it's a well-known story."

"Oh, it is."

"Do you know when it happened, like what year?"

Dan stood up straight. "A little over fourteen years ago. It was in '82, early in the year. January, I believe."

Dunbar nodded. I had the impression now that perhaps he already knew some of the story and was comparing versions. He asked, "How did he die? I understand he was killed, but I wonder how."

Dan took in an audible breath through his nose. "The first story that came out of there was that he had been lynched, which would fit for a horse thief, but there weren't any trees tall or stout enough for that."

"We didn't see any today."

"You can't hang a man from sagebrush or a chokecherry bush. Oh, I suppose you could hang him from the peak of his

35

cabin. They hang 'em from barns and telegraph poles. But, anyway, no one hung him. They found him dead on the ground with two bullet holes in him."

"Do you think he was a horse thief?"

Dan tightened his mouth. After a few seconds, he said, "My opinions don't matter much."

Dunbar shrugged. "I don't have any reason to repeat them. I'm just curious."

"Do you want to know what I really think?"

"Sure."

"I don't think he was."

CHAPTER THREE

The boss squinted as he rolled his second cigarette of the morning. The haze hung low in the bunkhouse, as Bob and George had each smoked a cigarette as well. Dan had fried up a mess of bacon to begin with, so the wisps from the skillet contributed to the cloudy atmosphere, as did the kerosene lamp, which sent up smoke and fumes until George trimmed the wick. My coffee cup was empty, and I felt like going outside for a breath of fresh air, but I held my seat and waited for the day's orders.

The boss lit his cigarette and shook out the match. "Bob and George, you can go ahead with what's next on your sequence. You know what to do."

Bob was bent over, lighting a cigarette from the flame of the lamp. He drew back and nodded his head as he blew out a stream of smoke sideways.

George kept to his chair and tipped his head side to side, as if he was waiting to hear what the boss had in mind for the other half.

Bob stood up with his cigarette in his mouth and shook his arms. "We might as well get goin'."

George stayed put.

The boss rubbed his nose and said, "Bard, I need to send a note to Crowley. But I want you to go by Pearson's first and see if Bill's wife needs anything."

"She might be gone by now."

"Well, if she is, you can find that out. Dunbar can go with

37

you. Not that it takes two to deliver a message, but he can see a little more of the country, and I think it's safer with two."

George opened his eyes wider. "What's so dangerous about Crowley's?"

"Nothing that I know of. But a man was killed over there where they're goin' first. It's no trouble for me to send someone along with the kid. That's one of the reasons we send men out in pairs to begin with, you know."

"But we split up."

"Of course you do. But you meet up every so often. That's the whole idea. Look after one another."

"Yeah, yeah. I know." George stood up. "I'm not complainin'." He and Bob put on their hats and went out to their work.

The boss took a drag on his cigarette. "You'd think goin' to Crowley's was some kind of a prize."

Dan said, "Oh, you know George. He likes to gossip with the other punchers, trade doodads, come home with a new pocket-knife."

"Well, there'll be time enough for that. We've got the corrals to build, and roundup right after. Though I don't think I'll send him and Bob to work on the corrals." The boss turned to me. "Are you boys ready for today's chore?"

I said, "As soon as I have the message."

"Oh, yes. Here it is." The boss reached into his vest, took out a sealed envelope, and handed it to me. "You'll probably be at Crowley's at about the time they ring the dinner bell, so don't be shy. At least his grub's good."

The sun was clearing the hills in the east when Dunbar and I rode out of the ranch yard. I had saddled a red dun for the day, and Dunbar had fitted out a sorrel. The horses blew and snorted in the cool morning, so we let them move at a brisk pace.

The day was warming up when we rode into the Pearson

yard. The place was vacant and still, with no chickens or livestock about. The front door was closed, and the doorknob was tied with a piece of telegraph wire to a nail that had been driven into the doorframe.

"Looks like she's gone," I said.

Dunbar nodded. He was studying the house, yard, and animal pens. "It's not easy makin' it in a place like this, even when things are fair."

A slight movement of air tumbled a chicken feather in the dust, and my horse sidestepped.

"Wish 'em the best," said Dunbar.

I had a sense of how little a person's life could come to, with Bill Pearson and his wife packed up and gone, and I recalled Mrs. Pearson's complaint about people not wanting to put themselves out when something unjust happened to unimportant people. It all seemed rather forlorn as we lingered in the abandoned homestead.

A magpie came floating over the house and into the yard. Seeing us, it veered and flew away with a zigzag and a dip. We rode out of the yard with the sun at our backs.

Away from the chalky buttes, I turned and headed us north toward Borden Crowley's ranch, the BC. Our route took us across a broad grassland once again, not unlike the trip we had made the day before. On the way to Bancroft's, I had detoured us to the right to go past Blue Wolf Spring. Now the spring lay on our left, to the west, on the other side of a broad swell in the landscape. I did not see a reason to pass by that way again so soon, so I held us on a straight course toward the BC.

The melancholy feeling I had picked up at the Pearson place began to fade, but it was not replaced by happy prospects of friendship and frolic at the BC. I did not care for Crowley, from the little I had seen of him, and I did not know any of his men well enough to have friends among them. I might even say that they had a tendency not to be congenial with outsiders. But a job was a job, and I had a bit of pride that Lou Foster had entrusted me as his messenger, even if he felt he had to send along a bodyguard.

The sun was reaching its slow span overhead when we rode into the BC headquarters. The place had not changed since my last visit. The ranch house stood by itself, straight ahead, with fifteen-foot trees growing around it. On the left, a large, whitewashed barn with a hayloft and pulley track rose up above the stable on one side and the corrals on the other. Across the yard, on our right, sat a long building that combined a cookshack with a bunkhouse large enough for twenty men. The trees around the ranch house were the only ones in view. The rest of the place was dry and dusty but clean.

The bunkhouse door opened, and the cook stepped out to look at us. I recognized him from before, a balding man with a fringe of dark hair. His eyes drifted over Dunbar and settled on me.

"We came with a message from Lou Foster," I said. "Is your boss around?"

"He should be here in a while. He's out with the foreman. You might as well come in for a spell, give your horses a rest."

I glanced at Dunbar, who gave a mild shrug. "I suppose so," he said.

Once inside, we found ourselves at a long table with benches on either side.

"Have a seat," said the cook. "I'm workin' on the noon meal. You ought to plan to stay for it."

"We might," I said.

Dunbar and I took seats across from one another at the end of the table. Dunbar took off his hat and set it next to him, and I did the same.

Before long, the room brightened as the door opened. Two

men walked in. I recognized them as Fred Mullet and Boots Larose. They hung their hats and came to stand near us.

Mullet had straight, light brown hair and a sparse mustache of similar color. He wore a loose-fitting gray shirt and a sagging brown vest. He had his mouth open and his eyebrows raised.

"Hullo, kid. Seen them horses outside, and I thought it might be you."

I stood up, shook hands, and introduced him to Dunbar.

Larose stepped forward and said, "Birdy-birdy."

I took that to be his nickname for me. "Top of the day, Boots," I said. I shook his hand and introduced him to Dunbar as well.

After they shook hands, Larose put his thumbs in his belt and stood back. He had dark blond hair with a mustache and chin beard to match. He wore a yellow bandana, a tan shirt and vest, and denim trousers. His brown holster and yellow-handled six-gun hung on his hip as usual. He curled his lip and said, "Well, what's new?"

"Not much. Came to deliver a letter."

"Must be a big one. Takes two to carry it." He smiled. He had ears that stuck out, a prominent nose, and yellow teeth. His fingers had stubby ends, but he had a lean build with slender legs. He wore long, dark brown boots with mule-ear tabs, and he kept his trousers tucked in. His boots were dusty at the moment, and although he usually kept them shined, he had a general filmy quality about him whenever I saw him.

I said, "The boss sent Dunbar along so he could get to know the country."

"That's one thing about the boss. He's always the boss, and the rest of us is just nee-groes."

Dunbar's face tensed for a moment. Neither of us said anything.

Larose did not have trouble filling the empty space. "Are you lookin' forward to spendin' a while in town?"

"I haven't thought much about it," I said, though I assumed he meant the corral project.

Mullet chimed in. "You might think more of it once you're there. Though the last I heard, you still have to go to Ashton to find you-know-what."

I was saved from having to answer or ignore him. The door opened, and a man I did not know stepped inside. He was below average height and wore a close-fitting, dusty black hat with a narrow brim and a creased crown. He had a clipped mustache, brown like his hair. He had dark blue eyes that fell on me right away.

Mullet said, "These two fellas ride for Lou Foster."

I saw that he was speaking to a second man as well. Borden Crowley had stepped in behind the shorter man.

Mullet continued. "This here's Dick Ainsworth. He's the foreman. And you know the boss. At least you do, kid."

I shook hands with Ainsworth and Crowley. Dunbar, standing, reached across the table and did the same. Ainsworth bore down on Dunbar as he did with me, but Crowley's brown eyes did not settle on us as he went through the motions of shaking hands.

Ainsworth moved his dark blue eyes toward me as he said, "What brings you boys here?"

I drew the envelope out of my vest. "Lou Foster has a message for Mr. Crowley." I reached past Ainsworth and handed his boss the letter.

Crowley took the envelope with an uninterested expression and tucked it into his jacket pocket. "Thanks," he said. "I'll get to it right away."

As he took off his hat, I renewed my impression of him. He was taller than average, with a self-assured air. He had a full head of hair that was a mixture of mousy light brown and a dull gray. It had a waxy sheen to it, as it lay flat where his hat had been. His hair was trimmed, and he was clean-shaven as always. He hung his hat on a peg and said over his shoulder, "Let's all sit down. There's more coming in."

Crowley sat at the far end of the table, withdrawn into himself, it seemed. Ainsworth sat in the middle, while Mullet and Larose sat closer to Dunbar and me. I had not seen a washbasin, and no one else took the trouble to wash up, so I imagined they saved that ceremony for the evening. Meanwhile, the aroma of fried beef drifted on the air.

The cook set a stack of plates in front of me, so I passed them down, one by one. Next came a crockery vase of knives, forks, and spoons, so I sent it along as well.

More men came in, and by the time the cook had two platters of meat on the table, I counted sixteen of us sitting on the benches. Fried potatoes came next, followed by eight tin plates of biscuits.

The meal proceeded with very little talk. The click and clack of knives and forks predominated, with an occasional request to pass the biscuits or the salt.

When the meal was over and the men sat drinking coffee and smoking cigarettes and pipes, Mullet spoke up.

"Well, Dunbar, how do you like this country? Have you been here before?"

"I like it fine, and I have been here before."

Everyone at our end of the table, including myself, paid attention.

"About fifteen years ago, when I was first out seeing the country."

"How do you find it now?"

"Much the same, though I believe I see more windmills now."

Boots Larose said, "You probably do."

Dunbar gave him a brief nod and returned to Mullet. "It's a

43

good part of the country to come back to, and I'm glad I'm here." Dunbar paused. "One thing I remember from before is a song I heard. I remember just a snatch of it, but I've always been curious to hear the whole thing again."

"How does it go?"

"Oh, it's not much."

"Come on."

"I don't want to hurt anyone's ears."

"Oh, come on, now. Sing it. Maybe someone knows it."

Dunbar moved his mustache up and down. "Maybe I will. Like I say, it's just a little bit." With that, he sang in a tolerable voice.

> *Meet me tonight in the moonlight,*
> *Leave your little sister at home.*
> *Meet me out back of the churchyard,*
> *Don't leave me to wait all alone.*

"Sounds familiar," said Mullet. "Seems to me I might have heard it. In a saloon. Most probably in a saloon."

"What does it matter?" said Ainsworth, frowning.

With his hat off, gray flecking appeared in his hair and beard, and he had a more visible thickening around the head and neck, the type that comes with age. His neck was also made to look shorter because of a knotted blue neckerchief. He wore a collarless dark blue shirt and a dark brown vest, with the yellow drawstring of his tobacco sack hanging from his vest pocket.

Mullet had a simple smile on his face. "It's interestin' to me."

Dunbar said, "It is to me, too. I've taken an interest in songs. You might say I'm a collector. Some people collect insects. Others collect arrowheads. I go for songs that are not well known. Like this one."

He sang again, in a voice that was not painful to the ear.

Where the Niobrara wanders
On its journey to the sea,
My mind drifts back in memory
To thoughts of you and me,

When the silver dew of springtime
Lay light upon the land,
And love was free and open
'Tween a woman and a man.

He said, "I'd like to know more about it, including who wrote it."

Ainsworth shot out a stream of smoke. "I don't know how much any of it matters, including who wrote what. For my part, all those songs are the same, caterwaulin' about someone who died of a broken heart or a broken neck."

I wondered if dying from a broken neck, in his terms, meant being thrown from a horse or being hanged. But I was used to being treated as a kid, so I let the conversation go back and forth in front of me.

Ainsworth had lifted his chin and now regarded Dunbar with what seemed like a disputatious air. At the same time, I was sure that Borden Crowley had heard some of the conversation, though he seemed to take no interest in Dunbar.

"Well," said Dunbar. "Here's part of what's got my curiosity. This second one I sang, about the Niobrara, I wonder if it's borrowed. I wouldn't say stolen. Just borrowed. It sounds like another song I once heard." He paused, but before anyone else spoke, he went on. "You see, I think I might like to make up a song myself someday, and I would want to be careful not to steal someone else's words or ideas."

"Good luck," said Ainsworth. "None of it is very original. Furthermore, any muggins can do it. He doesn't even have to know how to sing or how to play an instrument."

"That's in my favor," said Dunbar. "Reminds me of the fella who asked his bunkhouse pals if they had any requests for him to sing. One of 'em said, 'Over the hills and far away.' "

Ainsworth held his mouth firm.

Mullet was undaunted. With his voice rising, he said, "What is it that you want to know? I've been here since the days of the Cheyenne-to-Deadwood stage."

"I'd like to know more about these songs," said Dunbar. "Especially the second one, and who wrote it. What year did you come here?"

"In '84."

"I believe I heard these songs when I first came through here in '82. Fourteen years ago, almost fifteen."

"Could be," said Mullet. "That second one, I don't remember ever hearing it at all." He shifted in his seat and directed his voice to the other end of the table. "Say, boss, you were here in '82, weren't you?"

"Of course I was. What of it?"

"This fellow wants to know about a song he heard back then. Heard it here."

Crowley shook his head. "I don't know anything about any songs."

"No one does," said Ainsworth. "Why don't you just forget it?"

Mullet returned to Dunbar. "I know someone you can ask. He was here back then. He remembers everything he's ever seen or heard. You'll prob'ly meet him, anyway, if we go to work buildin' them krells. His name's Del Bancroft."

I flinched, but I didn't think anyone noticed.

"Thanks," said Dunbar. "Doesn't cost anything to ask."

"And no harm," said Mullet.

Ainsworth snuffed out his cigarette and swung his leg over the bench. Several of the other men followed suit, and the company began to break up. Dunbar stood up as well and turned to say thanks to the cook. When his back was turned, I felt a touch at my elbow. I was still seated, so I had to look up into the face of Borden Crowley. As before, his brown eyes did not quite settle on me. He stood close, so he did not have to speak loud.

"Tell your boss I'll send him a message back. When I get a chance."

"Very well," I said. Because of his closeness and my perspective, I had a close-up view of his gold watch chain, shining against the background of his silver-gray vest and jacket. A second later, he was gone.

His manner struck me as abrupt and evasive. I do not think it would have seemed any less normal if he had told me straight that he did not want someone like me to carry a message of his.

My impression lasted but a moment. Dunbar and I put on our hats and walked out into the bright sunlight. We watered our horses as the BC riders saddled fresh mounts for the afternoon's work.

When we were a half-mile out on our ride, Dunbar said, "Lou was right about one thing. The grub's good."

"I wish I could say something similar about our host. I've known him to talk down to the likes of us, but this time he all but snubbed us."

Dunbar laughed. "I don't think he would like to hear me saying this, but I thought he made himself pretty clear, in spite of his efforts not to."

Whatever Borden Crowley wanted to convey in his message did not take him long, for Boots Larose showed up at our bunkhouse that same evening while I was washing my hands and face before supper.

Lou Foster was already seated at the table, so Larose strode over to him and handed the envelope with a bit of a flourish.

"Thanks," said the boss. "Supper's on the way. Go ahead and get cleaned up."

Larose hung his hat and stood behind Dunbar, who was behind me. "Just a little message," he said. "Took only one of us to carry it."

I stepped aside to dry off and let Dunbar move forward. "Did you see any snakes on the way over?" I asked.

"Nah. Last one I saw, I shot his head off." He patted his holster.

Dunbar straightened up and took the towel from me, but he did not move away from the basin. He dried his face and mustache, then smiled and said, "I don't know how true this is, but I heard a story about a fella in Texas, I believe. He killed a snake by stompin' on it, but it bit through the sole of his boot, and he died. His brother inherited his boots, and the first day he wore 'em, he died, too."

Larose said, "I think that's just an old wise tell."

I was sure I heard him correctly. Dunbar's eyebrows tensed with a curious expression, and he stepped aside to let Larose move up to the basin. "I don't believe half the stories I hear about snakes, anyway. I believe yours, of course."

Larose made quick work, washing only his hands. He turned and took the towel. "How about wakin' up in the mornin' and findin' a rattlesnake coiled up in your fryin' pan? You'd better believe that one, because I've seen it."

Dan's voice carried from the end of the table, where he was setting a stack of plates. "That's why you should turn your skillet upside down."

"I do that, too. This was in someone else's camp."

As the boss smoked his cigarette after supper, he said, "You might as well stay over, Boots. You don't want to ride back in the dark. Have your horse step in a hole."

Larose had pushed away from the table and sat with a long boot hiked up onto his knee. He had spilled a few grains of tobacco while rolling his cigarette, and he brushed them onto the floor. "Might do that. Thanks." He struck a match and lit his smoke.

"That's good," said George. "We have enough for a little contest."

Bob said, "Don't listen to him, Boots."

Larose blew smoke through his nostrils. "What contest?"

"Boxing," said George. "We've got two pair of boxing gloves, and we haven't used them all season."

Larose spit a fleck of tobacco at the floor. "Who are you tryin' to get me to fight?"

"This isn't fightin'. This is sport."

"I don't want to beat up this kid."

"No, we leave him out of it."

Bob said, "You can leave me out of it, too."

"No, no," said George. "There's four of us. We draw straws. The two short straws go first, and the two long straws go second. Then the two winners go at it."

Larose said, "I need to put my horse away."

"Well, hurry up. We've still got daylight." George spoke to Dunbar. "You're game, aren't you?"

"It's just a sport, isn't it?"

"Sure."

"All right. Count me in."

Larose sniffed. "What's the prize?"

"Each fellow can put up, let's say, four bits. Sweeten the pot."

The boss said, "I'll add four bits. How about you, Dan?"

"I suppose so."

Everyone looked at me. "Sure," I said. "I will, too."

Larose said, "I don't have any money on me."

"That's all right," said George. "We've still got three dollars. That's two days' wages and then some."

"Let me finish my cigarette."

Dan pulled two straws out of his broom, and we made two short ones and two long ones. I held the straws while the four contestants drew. Bob and Dunbar drew short, and George and Larose drew long.

"Hurry up and put your horse away," said George. "I'll get out the gloves."

The sun had set and dusk had not yet drawn in when Larose returned from the barn. I noticed that he was not wearing his gun belt. No one from our outfit was wearing a hat. Bob and Dunbar had their gloves on and were standing outside the bunkhouse. Dan and the boss were seated in chairs against the building.

Bob had an uneasy look on his face as he asked, "What are the rules?"

George said, "Fight fair. Go until someone gets knocked down or has had enough."

Bob took a deep breath and stepped around to face Dunbar. He held up his gloves and peered over them.

Dunbar held his gloves at chest level. He led with his left foot and jabbed with his left hand. When Bob moved back, Dunbar moved in with a right and did not hit him very hard.

Bob dropped to the ground on his right side and held up a glove as if he expected to be hit again.

"That's enough," said George. "See? No one gets hurt." He helped Bob to his feet, took his gloves, and handed them to Larose. Dunbar handed the other pair to George.

When George had his gloves on, he put his elbows forward and curled the gloves back toward his nose. He began to prance, and I could see that he thought of this whole contest as a show.

Larose, who had taken off his hat and set it aside, put his gloves up in similar fashion and began to hop around, clumping his boots on the hard ground. He seemed to be in the spirit for a show as well.

The two of them bounced back and forth, feinting, until George landed a blow. Larose's head shook, and his hair seemed to stand out straight. He came back flat-footed, no longer dancing, and held his gloves at waist level. He circled to his right and then to his left. George was moving his head from side to side, as if he was looking for an opening. Larose was watching his opponent's gloves but was keeping an eye on his feet as well. I saw why. As soon as George crossed one foot over the other, Larose moved in and clobbered him.

George landed on the ground sitting up. He held a glove to his jaw and said, "By God, you caught me off guard with that one. I guess you win."

Larose said, "Fist-fightin' is nee-gro stuff where I come from, but you say this is sport, so I go along. But I don't know anything about it."

I didn't believe him about not knowing anything, but I didn't think his claim would make Dunbar any less cautious. It might give Larose an excuse for losing, though.

The first two rounds had gone so fast that we still had light. As Dunbar and Larose squared off, they made an interesting contrast. Dunbar, a little taller and darker-haired, was as husky as a buck deer. Larose, lighter-haired and lean-legged, might have reminded a person of an upright wolf in an illustrated fable.

Larose did not prance this time. He stalked, planting one foot and then the other, moving to the right and to the left. Dunbar moved with him but did not cross his feet.

Larose lunged in, swinging like a windmill, and Dunbar stopped him with a punch that shook his hair again. Larose stepped back, then rushed. He ducked under Dunbar's gloves and wrapped his right arm around Dunbar's waist. I thought he was going to step behind and trip him, but Dunbar sprawled back, broke free, and clubbed Larose on the ear.

"Fight fair," said Dunbar as they separated.

"We're not fighting." Larose now began to hop around, moving forward and backward and shifting in a circle to his left.

Dunbar met him, and the two men exchanged short punches. They separated, and I could hear both of them breathing. Larose tried another rush, and Dunbar hit him one-two, enough to shake his hair and knock him to the ground.

"That's it," said George, stepping in. He bent to help Larose up. "You're not hurt, are you?"

"Oh, no. I'm fine."

"See? No one got hurt. Just like I said."

"Yeah, but I wish I'd thought to take these boots off. They wore me out. And I had to fight longer in the first round than he did."

"None of this was a fight."

"You know what I mean."

"Oh, yeah. I agree with you. Come on into the bunkhouse, and you can take your boots off."

"Nah. Now that I think of it, I should go back this evening after all. I've got an important job I should start first thing in the morning."

"You're not sore, are you?"

"Oh, no. and I've got a good moon to travel by. I actually like it that way. Let me find my hat."

When Larose was gone and the rest of us had moved indoors, Dunbar washed his face again.

George said, "You don't look too bad. How do you feel?"

"Oh, I'm all right. But I'd like to say one thing. I'd just as soon everyone keep their money."

"But you were the winner."

"I know. But like you say, it was all for sport."

CHAPTER FOUR

Dunbar walked into the bunkhouse with an easy air after pitching his shaving water at the base of the little elm tree outside. Bob lay on his bunk with a red handkerchief over his face. George was sitting on the edge of his bunk, cleaning and oiling his six-shooter. I sat at the table, feeling my jaw and thinking I would shave, also. The day being Sunday and a day off, the bunkhouse had a calm, unhurried atmosphere.

Dunbar set the basin on the stand that held the mirror. He said, "Bob, you're not feeling the effect of that boxing match last night, are you?"

Bob pulled the handkerchief aside and said, "No. I have a headache, and my sinuses are all stuffed up. It happens this time of year when the sagebrush has all the little beads on it."

"Sorry to hear that."

"I'm used to it. It's just something I have to put up with until the weather changes. Frost or snow, or even a cold rain."

I poured water from the kettle into the basin and tested it with my hand. It was hot enough, so I dipped my brush into it and began to work up a lather from the soap in my shaving mug.

Dunbar had taken a seat at the table not far away. As I began to daub the lather onto my face, he said, "I was thinking it would be a good day for my horses to get some exercise."

I met his glance in the mirror and nodded.

He said, "If you'd like to go along, you could ride the

buckskin. He's a good packhorse, but he's also smooth to ride."

"Sounds fine," I said. "I didn't have anything else planned."

"No hurry," he said.

George looked up from oiling his pistol. "Don't cut yourself."

The air was warm and heavy when we rode out at about midmorning. I asked Dunbar where he would like to go, and he said north seemed like a good direction. I let him set the course, and before long I saw that we were headed in the direction of Blue Wolf Spring.

The sun hung straight overhead when we reached the spring. The clay bluffs looked like baked mud. The chokecherry bushes, dark-leaved and chewed straight across the bottom, did not waver. The old set of cow bones reflected the sunlight in a dull shine, as did the rectangle of stones that marked the old foundation of the horse trader's cabin.

Dunbar dragged his cuff across his brow. "Let's stop and give the horses a drink," he said.

I let him go ahead as the horses picked their way up the gentle slope to the mouth of the canyon. As on our previous visit, water was seeping over the edge of the wooden trough, and the ground was pocked with cattle tracks. Yellow jackets buzzed low and crawled in the indentations. Dunbar rode to a higher spot where the ground was dry before he dismounted. I followed and stepped down with the buckskin between us.

We loosened the cinches and let the horses drink. A couple of long-legged insects skittered across the surface as the horses made small eddies with the intake of water. The air was still and heavy up against the bluffs, and I could feel the sweat trickling down my back. I wondered how cool the water was. I dipped my hand.

"It's not that warm," I said. "I wouldn't mind splashing my face."

"Go ahead. I'll wait." Dunbar took the reins and drew both horses away a few feet.

I set my hat on my saddle horn, pulled up my sleeves, and bent forward. I rinsed my face, rubbed my eyes, and stood back.

Dunbar handed me the reins. In addition to hanging his hat on the saddle horn, he laid his riding gloves on the seat. He turned up his sleeves, lowered his face, and dipped in. He came up looking something like a walrus, at least as I knew walruses from pictures. He rubbed his mustaches and blew away a spray of water. He stood back and waved his hands to let them dry.

As he did so, I caught a glimpse of something I had not noticed before. A dark spot, perhaps made darker by the water, showed in the palm of his right hand. I had the impression that he had been burned there at some time. It did not resemble a scar as much as an old callus, the kind that I could remember acquiring when I pushed the tip of a shovel handle with the palm of my hand for an hour or more, cleaning corrals. Scars, as I knew them, were pink and sometimes white, but I also knew that dark substances, like pencil lead or gunpowder, could lie beneath the surface of the skin for a long time. I do not know why I thought he had been burned there, and I cannot remember if by that time in my life I had read of criminals and slaves being branded in earlier times, for identification.

The moment passed. I did not stare at the spot, and he did not make any apparent attempt to hide it. We led our horses away from the low bluffs and made ready to mount up. I put on my hat and tightened my cinch. When I swung aboard, I saw Dunbar already mounted, with his gloves on.

"Where next?" I asked.

"You wouldn't object to a visit at the Bancroft place, would you?"

"No," I said in a tone that I kept from being too enthusiastic.

"I wouldn't mind seeing the stagecoach again."

As we set out, Dunbar said, "Water is a mystery, isn't it? So much of it is underground, and we can only guess at what it looks like down there in its pools and currents. And why it comes up where it does—or disappears, as some streams do. There's a scientific explanation, but it still seems, at times at least, to be something that the water or some other force decides."

"It would be an interesting subject to study."

"Yes, it would. That, and the cycle of evaporation and rainfall, and the cycles of plenty and drought. A common puncher like you and me, we know that a thunderstorm can build up on a hot afternoon, or masses of snow can come down from the north, but it takes a great deal of study to know why those things happen."

"I'm sure it does."

"You take this part of the country here, where the wagon trains and the railroads have gone across. Pilgrims who come out here in a good year, they see grass growing up to their stirrups. So they decide to stay. They raise cattle and crops, and they take the good years with the bad. To all the optimistic ones, this is the Garden of the Lord. A benevolent place."

"I hadn't heard that term before."

"I didn't make it up. It's a common way of seeing the West, with its free land and opportunity. Some people emphasize the garden part more than the Lord, but others hold it like a creed, as if they're following the call. Some of them believe the rain follows the plough, and I think that takes some zeal. Then they follow through with the idea of work, work, work."

Thinking of people of religious zeal, I said, "I have known of some people who don't even cook food on Sunday, but they do tend to their livestock and chickens."

"Even Presbyterians have to be practical. Not to single them out, but I think they're the ones who don't cook on Sunday. At least the ones I've known. But I break bread with them, and the Baptists, too, though if there's any truth to the old jokes, you're more likely to be offered a glass of whiskey with the Methodists or a glass of wine with the Catholics. Just jokes, of course. All these religions are good, or at least their teachings are. By the way, I hope I didn't step on any of your ground."

"My mother's family was Lutheran."

"Well, they're good, too. Like I say, they all have good principles, even if some of the followers stray on the primrose path." He rode onward for a minute as if in thought, and he said, "Actually, I think I got off track myself."

"In what way?"

"About the garden. I meant to mention the other half. The people who don't see it as the Garden of the Lord think of it as the Great American Desert. The ones who see these drying grasslands, not to mention the deserts themselves, as something to travel across and put behind, or something to struggle against. Even a place to die. Travelers wander off into lost canyons or unending mazes, and the elements get to them."

"Like people in glaciers or drifts of snow," I offered.

"Yes. That's another aspect of it, seeing it as a wasteland or desert. The land is an adversary. Not benevolent at all."

"Which way do you look at it?" I asked.

"Hah. You can't have one without the other. It's like the Old Testament and the New Testament, sin and salvation. Though the land is neutral. It doesn't decide. It just is. But sometimes it's a garden, like we see it today, and at other times it's, well, you've seen the bones."

"Not human bones, that I know of."

"Well, they're out there, too. Some of them right where they fell, and some of them where they've been hidden. But even those are like the man in the glacier. Always there."

"Like old Alex Garrison. He's buried somewhere on his place, you know."

"Oh, yes."

I frowned. "Do you mean that you know it or that you agree?"

"Well, if he's buried there, in a sense, he's like the man in the glacier, but he's not like all the hidden ones."

"What's hidden here is who did it."

"The knowledge of it, yes. But I'm beginning to fear that I'm not being a good influence on you. Too morbid. We should be singing songs about Swiss milkmaids."

As we rode onward, I began to feel a nervousness. Emma would not expect me back so soon. I hoped she would be happy to see me, and I thought she would be, but I feared that she might have some other visitor. After all, it was Sunday, and I had no idea how many other young blades had an interest in her.

I wished I had thought of or found something to bring her, but the time had been short, and I had not gone anywhere new. Except the BC, I recalled. Perhaps if I had been more sociable, like George, I might have struck up a trade for some doodad. But that wasn't like me. I would have been happy for the moment with a pretty stone, the likes of which a person might find in a streambed. I had kept an eye out at Blue Wolf Spring, but all I had seen was mud. I did not think that the Niobrara River would offer much better. I imagined a mountain stream, clear and splashing over smooth boulders, stones, and pebbles. The scent of pine trees and campfire smoke . . .

"There's a nice one," said Dunbar. He drew rein on the blue roan, and the buckskin stopped with it.

A hundred and fifty yards to our right, a lone antelope buck stood against the background of paling buffalo grass. His dark, curling horns and his tan and white markings caught the full wash of sunlight. He stared at us for a long moment, then made a *whuff!* sound that carried across the distance. He turned, bending his knees and ducking his head, and raced away. He reached the crest of a low rise another hundred yards away, turned, and began walking.

"They know what kind of a distance to keep," said Dunbar.

"I've heard you can lure 'em in by waving a white flag."

"I've heard that, too, but I've never tried it. I've also heard you can lie on your back, lift your legs in the air, and wave 'em. I think you'd want to be by yourself if you tried it. You'd feel pretty silly when it didn't work. Even at that, you never know when you're alone out here in the big wide open."

"That's for sure," I said. "I don't know how many times I've had someone come up out of nowhere." I recalled the day I met him, just a few days earlier.

"There, he's gone again." The antelope had taken off on a run. "I wonder if he saw something." Dunbar shook his reins, and the blue roan moved ahead.

We rode on, and I fell back into my earlier thoughts about what kind of a gift I could find for Emma. I pictured the Niobrara, well behind us now, a treeless, bankless stream winding through the grasslands with very little water in it. In most places a traveler would not know where it was if it was very far away, and once he was there, he would see reeds and rushes and mud, with very few stones. Again, I had images of a cool mountain stream, with water so clear that I could see bluestone or redstone pebbles against grains of sand in the bottom.

A thudding of horse hooves brought my attention up and around to the right. Both of our horses stopped. Two riders were loping down a shallow draw toward us. As they drew closer, I recognized the long, dark boots and yellow bandana of Boots Larose. Half a length back on his right bobbed the narrow-brimmed black hat of Dick Ainsworth. The two men were riding sorrels that could have been matched for a parade.

They turned on a wide curve in front of us, and I thought they were going to ride past us. Larose raised a yellow-gloved hand in a wave. Then the two of them stopped short, their horses jolting and bunching up in a gathering cloud of dust. Both men were wearing six-guns.

Larose's stirrup was a foot away from mine, and he had a saucy expression on his face. "Where ya headed?"

"That way," said Dunbar.

"We can see that. We was wonderin' what you're up to. Looks like you're both dolled up for Sunday."

I could feel Ainsworth's eyes on me.

"I work every day," said Dunbar.

"So do I. Just like I told you last night. Got work to do." Larose nodded to Ainsworth, and they took off.

I thought Larose's stirrup would clear mine, but he must have moved the toe of his boot, for he caught the edge of my stirrup and twisted it. A pain shot up along the inside of my leg, and my horse turned with the force of the jolt.

I glared at the retreating riders. "I think he kicked me on purpose," I said.

"Did he hurt you?"

"Just for the moment, I think."

As we moved ahead, Dunbar said, "Antelope have good eyes. They've got their sockets out front the way they do so they can see around at long distances. An antelope stands on a high point like that one we saw a while back, and he can see better than a man with field glasses."

I wondered if he was making a roundabout comment. "Do you think Ainsworth and Larose saw us?"

"Could be. But if they really wanted to know where we were going, they could have hung back and watched. I wouldn't be surprised if they were moving right along, and our friend the antelope saw 'em. But you never know."

We rode on without further incident and made the last slow climb in early afternoon. As before, a light breeze met us as we leveled out on top. We waited for a moment for the horses to relieve themselves before we rode the last two hundred yards into the ranch. Gazing afar, I saw a few pine trees in the southern reaches of the Hat Creek Breaks. In the other direction, I saw the Rawhide Buttes, with dark Rawhide Mountain rising in the haze. Those formations had springs and trickles, but for a true mountain stream, I would have to go much further.

Ahead of us lay the Bancroft place, with the red and white buildings bright in the sunlight. One new detail was that a wagon stood in the yard, hitched to two dark horses that were switching their tails.

"Looks like company," said Dunbar.

That was my fear, until I saw that the wagon had a dark, square object sitting in it. What looked like two men, or a man and a boy, were untying ropes that had held the object in place.

We rode into the yard and dismounted. The tailgate of the wagon had been let down, and I identified the dark object as a sheet-iron coal bin with a slanting top and four knobby cast-iron legs. The two individuals who had transported it had finished untying and were putting the ropes into the back of the wagon.

I recognized the taller one first. He had a large, ungainly shape and leaned forward. He was not wearing a hat or cap. Though he was balding, I knew he was about my age. He had close brows, brown like his hair, and his eyes had a cloudy appearance. His name came to me: Otto Trent.

His companion was short and slight of build. In spite of the weather, he wore a lightweight jacket buttoned up to the neck and with his shirttails hanging out below. His trousers sagged low and bunched up over his clodhopper shoes. Like Otto, he did not wear a hat or a cap. He had tousled hair the color of old straw, blank blue eyes, and a few days' worth of stubble on his face. As he stared at me, I recalled his name as well—Carl Granger. Like Otto, he was close to my age.

The back door opened, and Emma stepped outside. She was wearing a gray dress and bonnet, and my heart skipped. She fluttered a wave at me and stopped to speak with Otto—loud enough, I thought, for our benefit.

"My father will be out in a minute. And look. More help arrived just at the right moment."

Otto spoke in his deep, slow voice. "I think the two of us can carry it, unless we have to go downstairs."

"We'll see."

The door opened again, and Del Bancroft stepped outside. "What, ho," he said, smiling. "Extra help."

"Glad to," said Dunbar. He handed me his reins and gave me a knowing look. "I don't think there's room for more than four of us to lay hands on that thing, so you can hold the horses. Water 'em if you'd like."

I stood back with the horses and watched as Del and Dunbar took over. With the help of the two lads, they scooted the coal bin to the back of the wagon, lowered it, and carried it to the house. Emma held the door open. When the last set of heels disappeared, she closed the door and walked toward me. I motioned at the water trough, and she fell in alongside me as I led the horses.

"Nice to see you again so soon," she said.

"It was Dunbar's idea to go for a ride. These are his horses."

She drew her head back and looked them over. "Nice-looking."

"Yes, they are."

"Warm day for a ride, just to visit."

"I didn't notice it. I was surprised to see someone here."

"Oh, Otto and Carl?"

63

"Well, yes. I didn't know the mercantile did work like this on Sunday."

"They were going to deliver it yesterday, but they had bad luck. One of the horses went lame halfway from town, and Carl had to take it back, riding the other one without a saddle. He came back with another horse this morning, and they set out again. Poor Otto had to spend the night alone with the wagon."

"Don't they wear hats?"

"Oh, yes. I think they took them off in order to handle that heavy coal bin."

We arrived at the trough, and I let Dunbar's two horses drink.

"Otto's the gentlest soul. We went to school together, you now."

"Oh. I didn't know that."

"He loves all kinds of animals."

"Is he the one who brought you a toad and a baby rabbit?"

"Oh, don't be mean. He's never brought me anything. This is the first time I've seen him in a couple of years."

"I'm sorry. But I have to admit I was afraid I'd come out here and see someone else on a Sunday visit."

"Ha-ha. Like Boots Larose?"

My heartbeat jumped. "Does he come by here?"

"He stopped to water his horse one day, and he passed a remark about you. But he's not my type at all, so don't worry."

"What did he say about me?"

"Nothing much. He asked me if I liked boys who were still wet behind the ears, like you."

I recalled what a petty thing he had done when he kicked my stirrup, and I realized I hadn't felt any aftereffects when I dismounted. "And what did you tell him?"

"I told him I didn't like any boys."

"I hope you didn't mean it."

"I think I did at the moment. He would make me not like

men or boys or anything. If I hadn't been out brushing my horse, I would have walked away and not talked to him at all. But I was stuck there."

I thought of telling her what Boots Larose looked like when Dunbar knocked him to the ground, but I didn't like the feeling I had when I thought that way. I said, "Well, I'm glad to be able to see you again. I don't know when I'll be back. I think Dunbar wanted to speak with your father, or I might not have visited today."

"I'm always here," she said. Her bonnet cast a light shade on her face. Her dark eyes met mine, and her pretty teeth showed when she smiled.

"I'll look forward to it."

The tan-colored nanny goat appeared from behind and crowded herself between Emma and me. Emma pushed against the goat's forehead and said, "Get back, Bridget. Don't be so pushy."

Sound carried from the house, and Otto stepped outside, followed by Carl. A few seconds later, Emma's father and Dunbar appeared.

Emma said, "I'd better go in." She brushed her open hand against mine, and she left. The goat followed. Emma called a farewell to Otto as she passed the wagon, and she went into the house. The goat wandered off to the edge of the yard.

I led the horses away from the trough as Otto brought the wagon horses around to drink. He was wearing a short-brimmed felt hat, while Carl at his side was wearing a large, floppy cap with a broad, short bill.

I said good afternoon to them, and they returned the greeting. Otto looked away, like the shy person he was, but Carl stared at me as before.

Del Bancroft and Dunbar walked at an unhurried pace toward the spot where I was standing. Del called out a thanks to the two delivery boys. Otto called back, "Thanks to you, Mr. Bancroft." Carl said something that I did not hear well.

Del smiled as he spoke to me. "Afternoon, Tag. Ridin' good horses?"

"These are Mr. Dunbar's. He's having me ride the buckskin today."

"He said he wanted to exercise them. Shall we go down to the barn where there's a bit of shade?" He was not wearing a hat, and the sun had passed overhead enough to cast a narrow shadow in front of the open door of the barn.

The three of us walked without speaking. Dunbar and I each led a horse, and Del Bancroft moved ahead of us at a quick pace. He turned and waited in the shade as we caught up.

"Nice to see your stagecoach again," said Dunbar, casting a glance at the interior.

"I haven't done any more on it since I saw you last, which was only a couple of days ago, now that I think of it." Del smiled, showing a good set of teeth. "Tell me what's on your mind."

"I'm a fellow of many curiosities," Dunbar began. "We've been past Blue Wolf Spring a couple of times, and I'm curious to know the story about the old horse trader who used to be there. I understand that you know all the history of these parts."

"Alex Garrison. Yes, he was a little odd. Reclusive might be the word. He lived there in a shack, and he used that narrow canyon as a pen for his horses."

"How long did he live there?"

Del took in a long breath. "More than twenty years. I remember him being there when I was a boy and would ride out with my father, and I believe he died when Emma was a little girl."

"Lived by himself."

"Yes. When I was a boy, I thought he was a wild man. He was

lean and long-legged. Wore suspenders. He had a long, gray beard and a wild head of hair. But that was just looks. He minded his own business and was civil to everyone."

"Yet someone killed him."

"That's true."

"Why do you think someone would want to kill him, other than the most obvious reason that he might have stolen, or been accused of stealing, someone's horses?"

Del winced. "When they found him, they also found horses in his corral that had a couple of local brands on them. One brand was Borden Crowley's, and I think people assumed that Alex was making light with Crowley's stock when he was gone for the winter."

"So no one pursued the case very far."

"Not that I recall."

"What do you think? Was he crooked?"

Del tipped his head to each side. "So far as to steal horses from a neighbor, I don't think so. Not to mention that it would be poor judgment to do something so obvious. And I don't think he was the type to be receiving stolen horses, in cahoots with someone else's operation. But he was a horse trader, and sooner or later, something might have passed through his hands. I don't know what other reasons there would be to kill a horse dealer."

"So you don't think he stole the horses in his corral."

Del shrugged. "I don't think he would do something like that, but they found the horses there, and that seemed to be a fact."

Dunbar said, "Maybe he wasn't killed for anything related to being a horse trader. On a broader scale, one man might kill another, or have him killed, over money and property, an old grudge, a new feud such as property lines, a woman, or to keep someone quiet."

Del made a long face. "Like I said, he didn't fight with his neighbors. The property lines on these homesteads and government tracts are pretty clear, although the deeds are not always in order. I think his was, because when his family members sold the place, there were no complications."

"Who bought it?"

"Borden Crowley. He bought it for the spring, and the land itself extended his range farther south."

"And that was the only property the old horse trader had?"

"As far as I know, yes. And Crowley paid for it, fair and square." Del looked up at the rafters and came down. "There was one thing that was not everyday ordinary, though."

"What was that?"

"People said that Crowley thought Alex had a stash of money. You know, there's a hundred stories about buried loot from the old stagecoach robberies, and people get the fever. Crowley had his hired men knock the shanty into pieces, tear up the floorboards, and burn it all. People also said he searched the canyon for traces as well. But I don't think, and I never heard anyone say, that the rumor of money would have been enough reason to kill someone."

"How about a woman?"

Del laughed. "Maybe you know more than I do, but when I think of a man who is killed over a woman, I think of someone who's good-looking, or has money, or is a smooth talker. Maybe all three. Alex was none of those. He was a dyed-in-the-wool bachelor, and he had a tendency to smell like an old billy goat. I don't know of any woman who took a romantic interest in him, or the other way around."

"So the idea of someone putting him out of competition in that way doesn't seem very likely."

"Not Alex."

"I think the only motive we haven't covered is to keep

someone quiet."

Del shook his head. "I don't know what that would be for. Alex kept to himself. Like I said, he minded his own business. He didn't go around and gossip."

"He doesn't seem like such a bad sort."

"Once you got used to his . . . eccentricities, he wasn't."

CHAPTER FIVE

The sun was bearing down on us in the hottest part of the day as we rode southward through the parched grassland. Here and there we saw cattle, which, with my memory of the lone buck antelope we had seen earlier, kept me in a positive frame of mind. I believe that having seen Emma improved my outlook as well. Otherwise, the rays of the overhead sun, the haze above the surrounding landscape, and the heat rising with the dust and the grass particles stirred up by the horse hooves might have made me think of the rangeland as a part of the Great American Desert that a person had to endure and travel across. Dunbar's horses also helped, as they kept their heads up and did not plod.

We watered the horses at the windmill where we had stopped on our previous return trip. The afternoon was stuffy and still, so the blades did not turn. As I was used to the creaking of a windmill, I noticed the absence of the sound. I dipped my hand in the water, and it was warm. As a general preference I did not drink out of windmill tanks unless I had to, as many of them, like the one at hand, were lined with green slime and jelly on the sides and had white skeletons of birds lying in the sludge in the bottom. I did take the opportunity to rinse my face, however.

Dunbar did likewise, though not with as much gusto as he did with the cool water of Blue Wolf Spring.

"Poor Bob," I said. "With this weather, I can feel a swelling and itching around my eyes. It makes me think how much worse he has it."

Dunbar smiled. "Makes the cold rain and the snow all the more welcome." He tipped his head back and shaded his eyes as he noted the position of the sun. "It's not that late. We have time to ride home by way of town if we wanted."

"Do you think so?"

"Only if you wanted. I would hope not to corrupt you with the prospect of a cool beverage."

"I had been thinking of sitting on the shady side of the bunkhouse," I said. "But your idea sounds at least as good."

We rode into Brome from the north, at that time of day when the shadows were beginning to stretch. The town itself was not very old, having come into being with the arrival of the railroad some ten years earlier, so the shadows came from buildings. What trees there were had not grown as tall as a man on horseback. They looked tired and dusty, and the leaves of some were already turning yellow. The town was laid out east and west, along the trail that ran parallel to the railroad. The Niobrara River lay a mile or so to the south, but it had so little water this far upstream that it would not have made an oasis, anyway. The town well provided for the people's needs, and I imagined that these trees received their water as the tree outside the bunkhouse did—wash water that had already served at least one use.

When we arrived at the main street, Dunbar said, "Let's find this place called The Bower."

"Oh, yes," I said, recalling that Mrs. Pearson had referred to it. "We'll turn left here, then left again on the next block."

We turned as I suggested. We rode past the mercantile and then The Missouri Primrose, both on our left. Dunbar stayed close enough that I did not have to raise my voice very loud.

71

"Say, do you think this saloon takes its name from the path you mentioned earlier in the day?"

Dunbar pursed his lips as he regarded the sign in our passing. "Could be. But The Missouri Primrose is a little more specific. It's a prairie flower that grows in this part of the country and blooms in the springtime. Of course, given its name, it grows farther east and south, as well."

"I don't know which flower you refer to."

"You've probably seen it. It has large white petals, not very rigid. They're yellow in other parts of the country, but the ones that go by that name here are white."

I shook my head. "I don't place it right away."

"I'm sure you've seen it. Blooms when the weather is still cool and moist."

I could picture the short green grass at that time of year, with the various white and blue and yellow carpet flowers. "So this place is named for a flower."

"Seems like it. But that doesn't exclude the other possibility."

"Leading people down the primrose path."

Dunbar smiled. "Or offering it to them."

After turning left off of the wide main street, we came to The Bower on the right. Compared with The Missouri Primrose, it was an unassuming place. A small sign with the name of the establishment hung from a wooden awning above the hitching rail. A large wooden sign covered most of the front window. On the larger sign, I saw a painting of someone's idea of a beer garden, with an arbor and vines stretching up and over a table. On the table sat two mugs of beer. Above the arbor I saw the words "The Bower," and below the table I saw, also in block letters, the words "Beer and Ale."

We dismounted, loosened our cinches, and tied our horses. There being no raised walk on the side street, we crossed the footpath and went inside.

A bell tinkled, and the room grew silent around us. We were the only people in the place. As my eyes adjusted to the interior after a day in the bright sunlight, I saw the furnishings for the first time.

As in other drinking establishments, a mirror rose behind the bar, with a dark wooden pillar on each side. However, I did not see bottles of liquor or spirits. Rather, I observed mugs and glasses on two shelves. The place seemed almost bare. On the counter in back of the bar, I made out four pasteboard cigar boxes, a few rows of small white drawstring sacks for cigarette makin's, and a couple of rows of tobacco tins. Glancing around to my left, I realized that strips of daylight came in from around the edges of the wooden sign that covered most of the window.

Movement on my right caught my attention, and a woman walked into the area in back of the bar. As if by habit, she took up a cloth from beneath the bar and swiped the bar top in front of us.

"What would you like?" she asked.

Dunbar answered. "We had in mind a cool beverage."

"Which I have. Would you like something pale or something dark?"

Dunbar turned to me. "Given the weather, I think I'd prefer something pale. How about you?"

"I don't know much about these things, so I'll go along with whatever you think is good."

Dunbar faced the woman and smiled. "Two glasses of beer, with a preference for whatever is coldest."

The woman took two tall glasses from a shelf at the base of the mirror and moved down the bar to a place where beer taps stuck out of the wall. There she poured two glasses with an inch of foam on each. When she set the glasses in front of us, I caught a view of her.

She had light brown hair, bluish-gray eyes, and a clear

complexion. She had her hair pinned up. She did not wear jewelry or rouge but rather had a plain appearance, with a lightweight gray jacket in addition to a gray dress. I would have guessed her age at about thirty-five, and although she did not wear garish or revealing clothes, her dress showed her full figure to advantage. I thought her proportions would be pleasing to someone her age or older.

"Thirty cents," she said.

Dunbar had a silver dollar ready. He laid it on the bar and moved it toward her. "We might have a second one," he said. "No hurry with the change."

I thought I saw a small wink, and the woman brightened in response.

"Take your time," she said. "No need to gulp and run like some of these punchers do."

"My friend is in no hurry, and I am even less so." With his left hand, Dunbar took off his hat with a small flourishing sweep and said, "J.R. Dunbar, ma'am, and at your service."

I took off my hat as well. "Bard Montgomery."

"You're quite the pair of gentlemen," said the landlady. "My name is Mary Weldon."

"A pleasure and a privilege," said Dunbar.

"Thank you."

Dunbar raised his glass, touched it to mine, and drank.

I took a drink from my glass. The beer was cool, not cold but refreshing all the same. Trying to think of something to say, I offered, "It's a pleasure to know your establishment. First time we've been in here."

Mary Weldon spoke. "This is a quiet place. Not much hub-bub. But it's decent, and it's honest. Of course, I'm not saying that others aren't."

"Of course," said Dunbar.

I was lingering on her words, or rather her voice. I thought she sounded somewhat weary, as if she might have been through some trials in her life and was glad to have settled in a place that she could say was decent and honest. I imagined The Bower as her version of coming west to seek a new lease on life, a garden of opportunity.

In a tone that sounded like routine courtesy, she said, "Do you boys work on a ranch around here?"

Dunbar tipped his head toward me.

I said, "We work for Lou Foster, out east and a little north of here."

She nodded, and I did not have the impression that she knew of Lou or any of his hired hands. That seemed normal, for not only had I not been in her place before, but I had not heard Bob or George mention it.

No one spoke for a moment. Dunbar seemed to be taking note of his surroundings. When his attention came to me, I said, "Ask her about the song."

He made a light frown, as if he didn't know what I was referring to.

"What song?" asked Mary Weldon.

Illumination showed on Dunbar's face. "I think he means a song I mentioned the other day. Actually, two different songs, or pieces of them. I heard them when I first came through this country several years ago, and I've never heard them since. And with each of them, I heard only a part. One song is about the Niobrara River, which isn't much of a watercourse here but becomes more of a river as it flows through Nebraska. It occurs to me that the song might have come upstream and thinned out like the river itself, and if I wanted to recover the whole thing, I might have to travel halfway across Nebraska to a place like Valentine."

"I don't know that part of the country." She gave a faint smile.

"It's been a while since I was there."

"And the other song?"

"I heard only a stanza. It was about a fella who wanted his girl to meet him by the churchyard and leave her little sister at home."

"Sort of a ditty, then," she said.

"Not the kind that sailors sing. As I recall, it had more of a sad note to it."

"Oh, there are lots of songs like that. Sad and dreary. Like the one about the miller's daughter, who waits for years by the millstream for the man to come back, and he never does."

"Wonderful sorrow," said Dunbar.

"Sing it," I said.

"The song about the miller's daughter? I don't know the words."

"No, the one about the churchyard."

"Oh, I don't—"

"You can't say you don't know it. You sang it the other day. That is, the one stanza."

"Sing it," said Mary.

Dunbar stared at his glass. "I've got to see if it'll come around."

Mary's eyes were shining. "Oh, come on. Just one stanza. Brighten things up with a little sorrow."

"Very well." Dunbar took a drink of beer, straightened his shoulders, and sang the stanza as before.

> *Meet me tonight in the moonlight,*
> *Leave your little sister at home.*
> *Meet me out back of the churchyard,*
> *Don't leave me to wait all alone.*

"Well, that was nice," said Mary. "Too bad you don't know the whole thing. I can't say I've heard it before, but I can't say I haven't. I've heard all sorts of things, from songs with fifty verses to fragments like that one, not to mention pieces of one song mixed with snips of another."

Dunbar smiled. "How long have you had this place?"

"Two years, going on three." She seemed to reflect for a couple of seconds. "How long ago did you hear that song?"

"Oh, quite a while. Almost fifteen years."

"You must have been a mere lad."

Dunbar suppressed a smile. "I could barely reach my chin to the top of the bar."

She laughed. "You boys have a lot of stories." To me she said, "You don't talk much."

"I'm just a mere lad. Still learning."

"To talk?"

"In places like this."

She laughed again. "You're doing well. Men who talk the most in places like this are the ones who make trouble or end up in trouble."

Dunbar put his hand over his mouth.

She said, "You know I don't mean you. I'm referring to the ones who talk long and loud. There's no harm in talking, if it's just regular conversation. That's what people come in here for."

I thought it might have been a good opportunity for Dunbar to bring up the subject of Bill Pearson, but he said nothing.

Mary spoke again. "I'll leave you gents to your conversation. I've got a couple of things to look after."

She reached under the bar and took out a clean white cloth, then turned her back to us and began polishing glasses from the shelf in back. She glanced at the mirror every minute or so.

Dunbar finished his glass of beer, glanced my way, and made a motion with his head that I interpreted as meaning he was ready to go. I drained my glass and stood up straight.

Mary turned away from the mirror. "Another?"

Dunbar rested both hands on the bar. "Not today, thanks."

She made a small frown. "There's nothing wrong, I hope."

"Oh, no. We've got a long ride, and if I drink too much, I might get woozy."

"Just a minute, then." She reached for the silver dollar.

"Please keep the change," he said.

Her eyebrows went up. "Are you sure?"

"Yes, indeed. And fear not. We'll be back."

"I hope you will."

"We'll look forward to it." He lifted his hat and made a small nod.

I touched my hat brim and followed him to the door.

As we paused outside on the path, the glare of the afternoon made me squint and blink. When my vision cleared, I saw two men riding away on sorrel horses. As they turned onto the main street, I recognized the riders as Boots Larose and Dick Ainsworth.

"Those two get around," I said. I recalled the kick from earlier in the day and was glad I didn't feel any more pain from it.

"I'd say. I saw two fellas sitting on the bench here, and I thought that was who it was. I couldn't see much through the border of the window."

As we moved toward our horses, I said, "Is that why you didn't stay for a second glass of beer or ask about Bill Pearson?"

He caught my eye and gave a brief smile. "It was why I was so shy about singing the song. I knew they'd already heard it."

We tightened our cinches, led our horses out, and mounted up. I said, "I thought the lady might have given you stage fright."

"She's all right."

"Oh, yes. I didn't mean otherwise."

"Nothing wrong with running an alehouse."

"Not at all," I said. "I thought she was very . . . courteous."

"Indeed. Maybe a bit sad as well. Like the miller's daughter in the song, who looks in the stream and sees that her hair is streaked with gray."

"I don't know it."

"Just a song."

We rode on for a minute until I spoke again. "I thought you might have found her interesting."

"The alewife? Oh, I might, if things were different."

After another minute, I said, "Do you mean if she was in a different station in life?"

"No, I meant something else."

I realized that I was teasing him in a way that he did not tease me, and for a moment I felt unappreciative. To make amends, I said, "By the way, thanks for the drink."

"You're welcome. Sorry we didn't stay for two, but those other jaspers took some of the pleasure out of it." He shook his reins. "There'll be another time."

We rode on, with the only sounds coming from the horse hooves and the saddle leather. The air cooled as shadows stretched out from the lowly sagebrush. I fell into thoughts about Emma, drifted, and came back to the moment. I realized I was hearing a new sound. Dunbar was whistling a song, and I guessed it was the one about the miller's daughter.

As we hung our hats on pegs in the bunkhouse and washed up for supper, Dan was clanging around in the kitchen. I could smell fried salt pork, and my appetite quickened. I recalled that we had not eaten anything since our late breakfast.

Dan set the crockery jar of silverware on the table. "You boys go out tomcattin', but you make it back in time for the dinner bell. I'd bet Bob and George are still sittin' in the saloon."

"I have no idea," said Dunbar. "We happened to pass through town, but I didn't think to check."

"No matter."

"I did have a chance to visit with Del Bancroft earlier, though."

"Well, you fellas git around."

"Not like some."

"And what does Del have to say?"

"I asked him about Alex Garrison. He said he didn't think the man was the type to steal horses or be in cahoots with someone who did. Nor did he squabble with his neighbors."

Dan nodded. "You seem to be takin' interest in that old business."

"I mention it because what Del says seems to confirm what you said earlier."

"It does."

"And I take interest in it because it might have something to do with what happened to Bill Pearson."

Dan gave Dunbar an appraising look. "Are you some kind of an investigator?"

"I'm a cowpuncher."

Dan had a noncommittal expression as he said, "That's good." After a couple of seconds, he said, "Del Bancroft is all right. If he tells you something, it's on the square." Dan cast a glance my way. "I'm sure you've had a good recommendation from Bard as well."

Dunbar shrugged. "Bard doesn't say much. Says he's still learning."

"Maybe he is. What did you learn today, Bard?"

I had to clear my throat and think fast. "One thing I've noticed is that Mr. Bancroft doesn't have any trees planted around his buildings."

Dan said, "Could be they don't grow well there. Or maybe he has to be careful with his water."

"This is a nice tree you're taking care of outside here," said Dunbar.

"It's coming along." Dan rested his eyes on me. "They say every man should plant at least one tree in his life. They also say it's a good man who plants a tree when he's old and doesn't worry about whether he'll ever sit in its shade."

"That's a good thought," said Dunbar.

"Hell, I've known old people who didn't want to plant a fruit tree because they didn't think they'd live to eat anything from it." Dan shook his head. "If I thought apples would grow here, I'd plant a couple of them. Not worry about whether I'd ever get to eat any."

Dunbar said, "They grow farther north, but you need the right variety and the right location."

"They might put on fruit in town. But I don't think they would do well out in this windblown, frost-bitten country. I've seen apple trees that grow but never produce any apples."

I had a fleeting thought of the last place I had visited in town. In my imagination, The Bower was more than an alehouse. It had a garden out back, where people relaxed in the cool shade of fruit trees and grape vines as soft talk and gentle music mixed with the bubbling of a fountain.

Dunbar and I went outside in the cool evening and sat with our chairs tipped back against the bunkhouse. Bob and George had ridden in at dusk, in time for a late supper. They sat at the table with Lou, who had joined us a little late and was now smoking a cigarette.

I had the odd sensation, which I had had before, of having heard my name spoken out loud and having thought that it sounded strange. I had known fellows with first names such as Ode, Dade, and Juve, and I wondered if they ever had such a sensation. Then again, I had had the same experience with a plain word such as *lunch* or *book*. If I played it over and over in my ear, without reference to anything else, it began to sound strange or foreign. Now as I sat with my chair tipped against the bunkhouse, I couldn't keep the word that was my own name from running through my head, as if it referred to something unrelated to me. Other words crowded in: *card, lard, fard*. I was sure I had read the word *fard* somewhere. And *canard*. My brain was beginning to whirl, as if I was thinking backwards in circles and was in danger of losing my bearings. I needed to break the spell.

I set my chair down on all four legs and said, "What about those heroic deeds you mentioned the other day?"

"Not sure what you might be referring to."

"You said those old poets sang about heroic deeds."

"Oh, yes. I believe I mentioned great tragedies as well."

"Yes, you did. Right now, I'm wondering what kinds of deeds."

Dunbar raised his eyebrows. "Regular stuff. Going to battle with sword and spear and shield. Facing the enemy. Or slaying monsters. Dying a noble death."

"I see." I took up the other half of the topic. "How about the tragedies?"

Dunbar drew in an audible, sniffing breath. "Well, it takes a special kind of story to be a tragedy. It's got to be more than just dying, like in a shipwreck. People write poems and songs about great misfortunes, but they're not tragedies in the purer sense unless someone makes a mistake and brings it upon himself. Otherwise, it's not that different from a caterwaulin' tale of a cowpuncher dying in a stampede." Dunbar rubbed his nose. "Then there's other kinds of catastrophes, like anarchists bombing a building. Nothing heroic about dying that way, and really not much tragedy. More treachery than anything else. And injustice."

"Then what makes the tragedy?"

Dunbar paused, as if organizing his thoughts. "A person coming to grief, partly because of his own error in judgment. And there's got to be something at stake, something bigger than himself. He can't just fall into a glacier. But if he's doing something bigger, like defending his country, and he knows he shouldn't cross the glacier, but he gets taunted into it—that's more like it."

I was enjoying the line of discussion. "How about dying for a woman?"

"Could be. Again, the circumstances have to be right. You know, the story has to be shaped right. If he goes into a burning barn, saves her, but dies in the process, maybe he's heroic, but it's not tragic."

"What happened to Bill Pearson isn't tragedy, then."

"No. It's injustice."

"And Alex Garrison."

"Probably the same, but we are yet to know."

"I guess I need another example."

"Of tragedy? Well, I don't have a ready idea about how to convert the fellow in the burning barn into a tragedy, so I'll go to one of the original stories. An ancient king of Greece wants to find out the truth at any cost, to solve an old murder and do away with a plague on the city. Turns out that without knowing it, he was the guilty one. He had killed his own father, who he thought was a stranger, and had married his mother, not knowing who she was. Total misery for everyone at the end." Dunbar's voice had a cheery tone. "Of course, that's the Greek view. Don't try to beat prophecies or defy the will of the Gods, and don't think you're going to be happy."

"Sounds rather gloomy to me."

"Oh, it is. In a wonderful way. But it seems as if I'm being a bad influence on you again. Much better to muse about good horses and pretty girls, eh?"

"I imagine, but don't you think we're supposed to know

about the dark and terrible things, not take the easy way?"

"Oh, yes, all that, and suffer, too."

He sounded so pleased at voicing these ideas that I couldn't help feeling uplifted as well. At the same time, in the back of my mind, I couldn't forget about Boots Larose kicking my stirrup. If he had done no more than that, I might have thought of it as an act of petty jealousy and bullying. But when I put it together with his keeping company with Dick Ainsworth and the two of them spying on us later on, I wondered if there was more to be known. As Dunbar would say, it was not tragedy, but it might be treachery.

CHAPTER SIX

Lou Foster leaned on his crutch and smoked a cigarette while Dunbar and I took turns grinding the coffee and double-bagging it.

"No sense haulin' beans and flour and salt and sugar into town when you can buy it there," he said. "But once you start working on the corrals, you might not have time to grind coffee."

"Twenty men to cook for," said Dan. "That's as much as a roundup crew."

"We've got only so much time. Or I should say, all of you do. The good thing is that your work camp stays in one place, and you don't have to pick up and move every day or two."

I assumed it went without saying that having a work camp was far less expensive than having to pay room and board for all the workmen.

Dan said, "Yes, and the bad thing is that all these men will be within walkin' distance of a saloon. They won't have time to grind coffee, but you can bet they'll have time to go look at the picture of the naked lady."

I had been in The Missouri Primrose, so Dan's words brought up a picture in my mind. In a large painting above the mirror in back of the bar, a woman with no clothes lay reclined on one elbow on a couch with only a thin, gauze-like scarf covering some parts of her.

Lou sniffed. "I think Crowley and his man Ainsworth will

work these men hard enough that they'll be mindful of gettin' their rest. After the first couple of days, anyway."

I grimaced. When I first heard of the corral project, I looked forward to the prospect of learning to work with milled lumber, to take accurate measurements, to plumb and square, and to build something durable. I thought it would be a step up from building pole corrals. But from the moment I learned that Borden Crowley would be in charge of the crew, I had a sense of dread. Having Crowley as the big boss and Ainsworth giving orders as well was unpleasant enough, but I was sure Larose would find his chances to swagger and bully.

"Too bad you can't be there," said Dan.

Lou held his crutch aside, stood on his ailing leg, and brought his crutch into place again. "If I get to moving around better, I will. But the way I am, I'll just get in the way."

Dunbar and I stood with the rest of the crew as Crowley and Ainsworth assigned men to their tasks. Two men went to laying out and staking the dimensions. Six were sent to measure and cut lumber. Four were told to begin building gates. Two men had the task of building sawhorses. That left four of us to dig holes and set posts.

With Ainsworth at his elbow, Crowley stopped in front of Dunbar and me. As usual, he did not look straight at us. He said, "You're Foster's men, aren't you?"

"That's right," said Dunbar.

"The two of you can work on post holes until someone says different." Crowley's eyes drifted in the direction of the other two men who were waiting. "Dick is in charge of digging the holes and setting the posts. As far as that goes, when I'm not here, he's in charge of everything. So you do what he says." Crowley turned and walked away.

Ainsworth lingered. To the other two men he said, "Start

hauling posts." He came back to Dunbar and me. "Get your tools. Every outfit was to bring a diggin' bar and shovels. Did you bring yours?"

"Yes," I said.

Ainsworth glared at me. "I was talkin' to him."

"Yes, we did," said Dunbar.

Ainsworth raised his head to address Dunbar. "As soon as Jim and Archie mark the first holes, get started. They'll tell you what kind of a post goes in, and that'll tell you how deep to dig." He brought his dark blue eyes back to me. "I don't want to see anyone loafin'. We've got a hell of a lot of work to do here, and not much time to do it."

I didn't answer. I didn't want to give him the opportunity to talk down to me again. Dunbar and I turned away and walked to the wagon for our tools.

I had not yet dug a foot down in my first hole when Ainsworth came by.

"You want to dig those holes straight down and on the spot where they're marked."

I nodded.

"And if Jim or Archie tells you to move your hole one way or the other, you do it. These posts are eight inches by eight inches, like railroad ties. They need to line up straight, and they need to be the same distance apart. How deep are you digging this one?"

"Three feet. They said the gateposts go down four feet, and all the others go down three."

"The corner posts should be deeper. I'll have to talk to them." He made a small spitting sound as if he was getting rid of a speck of tobacco, then made an abrupt turn and marched away.

Jim and Archie were not so bad to work under. They weren't the type to tell a person as little as possible. To the contrary, they would stop and chat with each man who was digging. They gave me an idea of how many pens and lanes there would be, and they pointed out where the catwalk would run down the middle, above the pens. Now I understood what the longest posts and timbers were for.

Jim also told me that Ainsworth did not know all that much about building corrals. His method was to go around and ask questions, gather information, and then come back and give orders as if he had been an expert all along. Jim said he had to tell Ainsworth not to haul all the posts to begin with because they would be in the way of running strings and piling dirt. So before long, four of us were digging holes.

When we had the first row dug, Ainsworth pulled two men from cutting lumber and put them to setting poles and tamping them in. They ran string to line the posts up straight, sighted in the tops for level, used plumb bobs for the sides, and tamped with an iron bar that had a knob on one end and a flare on the other. It was the first digging bar I had seen that had an end for tamping. I could tell right away that it was better than the tip of a shovel handle, which was all I had ever used.

When Ainsworth and Crowley were not around, I rather enjoyed being part of the whole project. I became interested once again in seeing how men measured, cut, squared, and fitted lumber. Everything had a logic and a sequence, and accuracy mattered a great deal.

Activity carried in the air. From where I worked, I could see the men working on the lumber pile. They sawed planks first to square the ends and then to fit for length. Boards thumped and clattered as men restacked the cut lumber. Dunbar dug two four-foot holes for the main gateway, then helped set the two twelve-foot posts. When the posts were tamped in solid, Dunbar moved on to dig more holes while the other two men took turns with a brace and bit. They bored one-inch holes for the bolts that would hang the gate. Then they nailed a ten-foot plank, a full two inches thick, on each side of the overhead span. Archie told me the nails were twenty-penny spikes.

The gateway stood like a monument by itself, but not for long. By midafternoon, a line of corral posts was tamped solid and ready, and men began hammering planks into place. Jim told me they had to tell Ainsworth not to cut all the corral planks ahead of time but to measure and cut as they went along. That part of the job smoothed out, and the shipping pens made of rough, gleaming lumber began to take shape.

I did not keep track of how many holes I dug. Rather, I abandoned my mind to the challenge of trying to make each one as close to perfect as I could. Sweat was dripping from my face, and I was shaving the sides of a hole I had already dug for depth, when Dick Ainsworth made one of his visits.

With no preamble, he said, "You need to go help the cook with the evening meal. He needs firewood. Find a wheelbarrow and haul him enough lumber scraps for tonight and tomorrow morning both." He made the spitting sound as before.

"Do you mind if I finish shaping up this hole?"

"It looks good enough to me. It's not a wedding cake, you know."

I found a wheelbarrow next to a wagon that held gate bolts, metal strap hinges, and kegs of nails. The barrow was an old, all-wooden affair mounted on an iron wheel with rusted spokes and a flat rim. The box had eight-inch slanted sides of cracked, weathered lumber, and I hoped it would hold together for as long as I used it.

I moved it to the scrap pile where four men were now measuring and cutting lumber. Mullet and Larose were working on a plank with diagonal cuts on each end, which I assumed would work as a brace on a hanging gate. They had the plank lying on a pair of sawhorses. Larose was sitting on the plank to hold it in place while Mullet was wheezing as he pushed and pulled on the saw.

As I set the wheelbarrow in place, Larose called out.

"Hey, kid. How do you like being a carpenter?"

From his jocular tone, I thought he was pretending that he didn't remember kicking my stirrup a few days earlier, or if he did, that it was all in fun.

"It's work," I answered. "I do my job."

"So do I." He moved his legs, as if he was a little kid on a bench or a swing. "What are you doin'?"

"Rustling firewood."

"That's good. Helpin' yer coosie?"

"People like their food cooked."

"I thought they had you diggin' post holes."

"They did."

"Well, like Dick says, it all has to get done. Back home when they had a work crew, they'd have a water boy come around with a mule. Water jugs on both sides. 'Course, gradin' roads, that's real work, and a crew of men goes through a lot of water."

I wondered where "back home" was, but I thought he might be looking for a chance to tell me what color the water boy was, so I didn't say anything. I began tossing blocks of wood into the wheelbarrow, hoping that the clunking sound would discourage him from going on. But he raised his voice.

"First job I ever had where I got to sit on my ass."

Mullet stopped sawing, so I paused in my wood-gathering. Mullet said, "Probably the first job where you ever got paid."

"What do you mean? I'd like to see you do some of the work I've done."

"I thought those road gangs were all prisoners."

"Maybe in your experience. In mine, there's whiskey and wimmen at the end of the day."

"Good luck findin' 'em both here. Whiskey, yeah, but for

women you got to go to Ashton."

"Hah," said Larose. "Wimmen are where you find 'em. You just need to know how to sniff 'em out."

I went back to tossing scraps of lumber, and Mullet took up the rasping and wheezing of his work. I positioned myself so I could keep my back on the other two, and when I had a cartload, I wheeled it away.

The scraps of pine lumber with fresh cut sides had a pleasant aroma. Once in the fire, they crackled and popped and threw out sparks. They burned hot and fast, and the coals did not last as long as some firewood did, so my pile of a half-dozen wheelbarrow loads dwindled to half its size the first evening. But Dan cooked a big pot of beans, baked about four dozen biscuits, and fried about fifteen pounds of beefsteak.

After supper, while the other hands lounged around the campfire, Dunbar and I washed the dishes on the tailgate of the wagon. Dusk had drawn in, and the night air was still and dry. We had our backs to the town, which had gone quiet. If the firelight had not reflected on the fresh planks of the corral some thirty yards away, I might have had the illusion that we had pitched our camp in the middle of the vast grassland, far from any town or the muddy trickle of the Niobrara.

"Not bad work, is it?" said Dunbar.

"Do you mean washing dishes or digging holes?"

"Either one."

"It's all work," I said. "I do find the building part of it interesting. You know, you see so many things that people build themselves, and some of them are crooked and uneven, while others are neat and straight. Sometimes I wonder what it takes."

"A desire to do things right, to begin with. Then, I suppose it takes patience, and a certain amount of dexterity. But first of all, I think it has to matter to do things with as much precision as possible. Then it gets ingrained with experience. That's my thought, anyway. I wish our friend Del Bancroft had been here to set the main gateway. It looks all right, but I think it could have been a little better. I understand he should be here tomorrow, though, so that should be good. Building the catwalk is going to be a little like building a house or a barn. If you say, 'Oh, that's good enough' at one point, it shows up at every step after that, and the error often grows."

"Is that how they set the gateway and arch?"

"Maybe a quarter of an inch out of square, and when they finished pounding in the spikes on the overhead, maybe a little more. But it stands by itself, not like the catwalk, so there's no real harm done. Just something to notice when you're up close in the process. Of course, I was working on the dirt detail, so I did what I was told." Dunbar rubbed at a spoon with his thumb, then dipped it in the dishwater. "Just part of a cowpuncher's life."

Borden Crowley did not show up the next morning. I realized I had not seen him since noontime the day before. Dick Ainsworth gave orders while the men were still eating their fried bacon and potatoes for breakfast. He assigned everyone to the same tasks as the previous day, with the exception that Mullet and Larose were now going to run string lines while Jim and Archie laid out the catwalk. I did not know what that meant for me until Ainsworth walked up to the spot where I stood eating at the tailgate.

He stood close and tapped me on the chest. His dark blue eyes bore down on me, and his clipped mustache moved before he spoke. "When you finish helping the cook clean up, Boots will show you where to dig the holes."

I nodded, releasing myself from his gaze and observing his creased face and his knotted blue neckerchief.

"The cook won't need you again till later this afternoon, so you do what Boots tells you."

I nodded as before, and he turned away.

I thought I was going to dig four-foot holes for the catwalk, but Boots put me to digging three-foot holes on one of the long outside rows. Jim and Archie had marked the location of each hole with a stake, and as I was digging, Mullet and Larose came by from time to time with the string line to keep the holes lined up. Meanwhile, Boots had Dunbar digging post holes for the catwalk. I thought Dunbar might have been assigned the deeper holes again because he was taller and stronger. I also sensed that someone might want to keep us apart, and I had a less definite feeling that someone wanted to subject Dunbar to the hardest work. To what purpose, I had no idea, but I knew it would not break Dunbar's spirit.

At noonday, he smiled as he fanned his face with his dark hat. I had the impression that he was playing a game with these fellows.

"Dig deep," he said. "You never know what you'll find."

"I've been hoping to dig up stagecoach loot with every hole, but the most I've found is a broken bottle and an old bent spoon."

"How about this?" He reached into his trousers pocket and brought out a reddish-brown object. As he showed it to me in his upraised palm, I saw that it was a figurine of a horse, etched out of a smooth piece of rock harder than sandstone. It had dirt encrusted in some of the striations.

"Did you find that here?"

"Dug it up this morning."

"That's nice."

"Take it. I'd like you to have it."

"Oh, no. You found it. It's yours."

"Ah, you know me. I move around too much to keep every

little thing I find. Take it. You might find something to do with it. Put it on a shelf or give it to someone."

Setting aside the question of how much I knew him, I took it in my hand, rubbed my thumb against the hard surface, and put the figurine in my vest pocket.

Dunbar said, "I expected Mr. Bancroft to be here by now. Maybe he'll show up this afternoon. I hope so. I'd like to see these posts and timbers as square as they can be."

I knew from the day before, as well as from prior experience, that the train stopped in Brome in the middle of the day. I was not surprised, then, when I heard the steam whistle hooting. I continued to eat my beans and biscuits as the train slowed in its approach from the east, passed behind the shipping pens, and came to a stop with a chug-chug-chug and a final hiss.

The small train station sat on the same side of the street as our corral project and work camp, and a hundred yards west. I did not expect Del Bancroft to step down from the train, as he would ride in from the rangeland in the north, but like anyone else, I was curious to see if anyone stopped off. My interest quickened when a woman in a dark traveling hat and gray linen duster stepped down from the second coach and looked around.

Dunbar appeared at my side where I stood by the tailgate. "Why don't you see if that lady needs help with her bag?" he said.

With Dick Ainsworth nowhere in sight, I felt free to do as I was asked. I set down my plate and left our camp area while all the other hands sat around and watched.

The woman turned to me and smiled as I approached her. I smiled in return, and when I drew within twenty feet of where she stood, I took off my hat.

After a few more paces, and seeing the station agent busy with the mail, I stopped and said, "I would be happy to help you with your bag, if you would like."

She smiled. "I would be grateful." She glanced to her left, and there, as if set by an unseen hand, sat a brown leather Gladstone bag.

Her bearing was so graceful that I made a half-bow. "Bard Montgomery. At your service."

She held out her hand. "My name is Medora Deville. I go by Mrs. Deville."

I took her gloved hand and pressed it, then met her eyes. They were dark and shiny, matched with her dark hair, which disappeared beneath the collar of her traveling coat. She had a smooth complexion, not pale, such as I have since associated with people from Mediterranean countries. I thought she had pretty lips as well, and I guessed her age at about thirty.

"To the hotel?" I asked.

"If you please."

I picked up her bag, which was broad and heavy, and lugged it along. As I headed across the street toward the Phelps Hotel, I felt the eyes of all the workmen watching. I said, "I wouldn't want to make a mistake. You said Mrs. Deville, didn't you?"

"Yes, I did. For those to whom these things are important, I am a widow. It's not always the first thing I tell people, but you look young and trustworthy. And sooner or later in a place like this, I have to mention it. To keep the wolves at bay."

"I understand." In truth, I understood but a part of it. "I hope you have an agreeable stay in this town."

"Is it your town?"

"In a way. I work on a ranch a few miles out. Right now, I'm working on a building project with all those other men." I was sure she had seen them looking at her. "Building a set of corrals."

"Oh. So that's what they're doing."

"Yes, ma'am." After a few steps in silence, I thought of

something to say. "Do you expect to stay in town long?"

"I can't say for sure. You might say I'm looking about. I've had experience in the restaurant and café business, and I'm somewhat looking for a place where I can buy or start a business."

"Are they expecting you here?"

"Not at the hotel."

I stepped up onto the sidewalk and rested the bag on the boards. "I'll carry it in. Just getting another grip."

At the entrance I let her go first. She opened the door for me, and I hauled her bag to the reception desk and set it down.

"Anything else I can do?" I asked.

"Not at the moment. I'd like to give you something for your efforts." She made a motion of raising her handbag with both hands.

"Not at all," I said, taking off my hat again.

"So gallant of you." She gave me her hand. "I'll remember you, young Mr. Montgomery. You've been kind."

"Thank you." With nothing else to say, I bowed and left.

When I returned to the work camp, I saw that Del Bancroft had arrived. He was standing and eating a sandwich made out of a cold biscuit and a piece of beef, and he had a cup of coffee nearby on the tailgate. Boots Larose, who seemed to have taken command in the absence of Dick Ainsworth and the higher-up Borden Crowley, was sending men back to their work. He stopped to visit with Del.

"Glad to see you made it. They say you're the man to be in charge of building the catwalk." Larose wagged his head as he smiled.

Del smiled in his easy way. "I can give it a try."

"We'll get started when you're ready. Just tell me what you need."

Del took a drink of coffee to wash down the last of his

sandwich. "I'm glad to see Mr. Dunbar here. I'd like him to help me."

The smile disappeared from Larose's face, and his head quit moving. In that moment, I had a sense that he was aware that he was speaking with Emma's father.

"If that's what you need, go ahead."

"And my young friend Montgomery, as well."

"I had him on another job, but if you need him, you can have him."

"If you don't mind. We all know each other, and I think we'll work well together."

In the course of the morning, Dunbar had dug eight four-foot holes, so we were ready to start setting posts. These posts were fourteen feet long, as they had to go into the ground, up six feet to the catwalk, and up above that for the railing. For each post, Del ran strings lengthwise and crosswise to position the post, plumbed it on two sides, and re-plumbed it during the tamping.

"We want these posts to be true and solid," he said. "Even at that, we've got to make sure we don't knock anything loose or crooked when we build up above."

Even though Del had the process well in hand, Larose and his understudy Mullet showed up every half-hour or so to look things over. Toward the latter part of the afternoon, they lingered and watched for a while. I thought Larose would look for a chance to ingratiate himself with Mr. Bancroft, but he took a different tack.

He gave me a taunting look and said, "Tell us about that woman you helped when she got off the train."

"I don't know what there is to tell."

"What's her name?"

"She said it's Mrs. Deville."

"Missus, huh? And traveling alone?"

I did not think it was my place to speak of her status in public, so I said, "I don't know everything about her."

"What brings her to this town?"

"I believe she might be looking for a business opportunity."

"Ohhh. What *kind* of a business?"

"She said she's had experience in the restaurant and café line."

"Oh. I thought it might be something else."

I was becoming impatient with him. "Why would you think that?"

"You seemed to move up right next to her. So I didn't know what kind of a business."

Dunbar spoke. "You shouldn't talk about things you don't know anything about."

Larose's eyebrows went up, and his face grew long with mock surprise. "Me?"

"Yes, you."

"I was just wondering."

Dunbar's voice had no play in it. "Yes, and your words are full of innuendo."

"That's a big word for me."

"I think you know what it means."

Larose's eyebrows drew into a frown. "Maybe I do."

"Then I think you should apologize."

"What for?"

Dunbar's face tensed. "For what you said, and the way you said it."

"Oh, go on. If there was anything out of line, it was in your way of thinking."

"We already discussed that."

Larose's eyes flickered to Del Bancroft and back to Dunbar. "You can't make me eat words that I didn't say."

Dunbar took a step forward so that Larose was an arm's

length away. "You had your chance."

Larose smirked. "I heard she was a widow."

I stared at him, my eyes wide open. He had already heard some gossip before he started needling me.

Dunbar said, "What does that have to do with it?"

"There's different kinds of widows, you know."

Quicker than I had seen him with the boxing gloves, Dunbar stepped forward and landed his right fist on Larose's jaw. Larose's hat tumbled away as he took half a step backward and fell to the ground.

He raised himself onto one elbow and rubbed his jaw with his free hand. He glared at Dunbar and said, "You might live to regret that, mister."

"We'll see," said Dunbar. "But don't press your luck with me."

Chapter Seven

Ainsworth sat with Mullet and Larose on the far side of the campfire that evening. Del Bancroft sat with Dunbar near the chuck wagon, where I took my meal standing up, ready to tend to any task that Dan mentioned. The other workers sat in groups of four or five. I was sure that anyone who had not seen Dunbar punch Larose had heard of it by now, and I was impressed by how well everyone acted as if nothing had happened.

The tone in camp was calm, and the men did not speak loud even when they had finished eating. I could hear the conversation between Dunbar and Del Bancroft without making an effort.

Dunbar said, "I understand you drew the plans for this set of pens."

"That's right," said Del. "When they asked me to contribute my share of the labor, not to mention the cost of the lumber, I said I would work on this project only if we had a set of plans drawn out. So that was my first contribution, the plans themselves."

"Good to have."

Del smiled as he pointed at me with his thumb. "When I was about this lad's age, I hired out to help a man build corrals on a ranch he had bought up north on Lance Creek. He had me and another young fellow, plus his father, who was old and gouty and heavyset. The father would move around slow and argue with the son about how to place the posts, maybe an inch or so one way or another, such as for gates he wanted to swing to block an alleyway and then close a pen. The father was right most of the time, but the son was stubborn. I don't know how many times we had to take out a post and move it an inch or two. Or other times, he would stand and scratch his head, trying to decide how he wanted the gate to swing and how he needed to get the three posts in the right places. At one point I asked him if he had a set of plans, and he pointed to his head and said, 'Right here.' I thought, that was a hell of a place for them."

Del looked at me, saw that I was following the story, and went on.

"From then on, any time I ever built anything, I drew a plan or a design first. It's not hard. Even for these pens, all I needed was a straight-edge ruler, a thirty-sixty-ninety triangle, a protractor, and a compass. Then when you have it on paper, it's a lot easier figuring your materials—how much lumber, how many hinges and bolts, and so on."

"It's a good skill to have," said Dunbar. "You learn these things when you're young, and you never know when they'll come in handy."

Del laughed. "Or you don't learn them. And you go ahead and build things, anyway. If I hadn't insisted, or if I hadn't worked on this project, they could have built these corrals as they went along. 'Play it by ear,' they say. Or 'The cows don't know the difference.' And in the end, they don't."

"Still, it's a satisfaction to do things well."

"Oh, yes. And it's a matter of degrees. Someone who builds a steam engine has to be much more precise than those of us who cut up lumber and nail it together. Then there's the fellow who builds a pole corral. He overlaps his poles, so he can be casual about his cuts. But he still might like to do a neat job, with all the posts the same height and all the cross-poles level. Needless to say, not everybody cares even about that."

Dunbar nodded. "You see all kinds. And it's not just a matter of who has money and who doesn't."

"That's true. People who are careless often end up with less money, but people who have money aren't always neat about the way they do things. By the way, I haven't seen Crowley. I thought he was in charge here."

Dunbar spoke in a lowered voice. "He is. But he seems to make himself scarce." Dunbar glanced toward the other side of the fire, where the BC hands were engaged in their own conversation. "Even his foreman disappears at times. But they might be working on some other aspect, like the accounts."

Del shrugged. "Well, it's not a steam engine or a battleship. Even with what's-his-name at third in command, the holes get dug, the posts go in, and the nails get hammered. And in the end, the cows don't know the difference."

In the end, I thought. For all the beef that was shipped, the big gateway led to the end. At one point I had thought it looked like a monument, but there was nothing ornamental. The new set of corrals, in this short period of time before a single plank would be splintered or a post would be knocked crooked, had a practical kind of beauty. But as Ainsworth had said of my post hole, it was not a wedding cake.

Borden Crowley arrived at the work camp in the morning while the crew was having breakfast. Wisps of smoke rose from the glowing coals, and steam issued from the spout of the big coffeepot hanging on the tripod. Crowley strode to the middle of the scene, and I thought he was going to pour himself a cup of coffee. Instead, he waved his arm at the gateway and hollered, "For God's sake, take that thing down."

Everyone turned to look. During the night, someone had hung a dead badger from the crossbeam and tied off the rope on a corral plank below. I had seen the animal hanging, as I was sure everyone else had, and I imagined it was someone's idea of a joke. I found it repugnant, but I hadn't put it there, and I assumed one of the men would take it down after breakfast. Now there was no waiting. Mullet sprang to his feet and hurried over.

Dan handed an enamel cup to Crowley and lifted the coffeepot from the tripod. "There's plenty of grub," he said.

"I don't care for any."

"Del Bancroft is here."

"That's good. Any problems so far?"

Dan poured steaming coffee into the cup. "None at all that I know of. You could ask Dick."

"I'll do that." Crowley turned and walked away.

Dunbar and I were carrying a fourteen-foot post to be set into position. With post holes and dirt piles in some places and corral posts standing up straight in others, we had something of an obstacle course to navigate. We had to weave around a spot where two men were lowering a corner post into a hole in a place where two alleyways intersected. Ainsworth stood by, giving orders as usual.

"Hold it straight up, free of the side, or you'll have to pull it back out and dig out the dirt all over again. There. Now, be careful and don't push too much dirt in at a time. These all have to be tamped in solid, 'specially the corner posts. Hey, look out, you. Stay clear of the men. One of these big posts falls over on you, it'll knock your brains out."

I thought he was talking to me, until I saw that a kid about sixteen years old had wandered onto the work site. He had blond, wavy hair sticking out below a short-billed cloth cap, and he wore drab work clothes with suspenders. He was carrying a knapsack, and I guessed he was a traveler. I had never seen him before. Catching sight of me at the end of the long post, he gave me a look of recognition, I imagine because I was the only other young person in view. He stood aside and then fell in and walked along with me until Dunbar and I stopped.

Speaking as if we were comrades, he said, "What's the chance of me gettin' hired on here? I'm tryin' to get to Montana, and I'm out of money."

I said, "The boss on this job is a man named Borden Crowley. I don't see him around very much."

Ainsworth spoke from behind us. "We're not hirin' anyone, kid. These men are all paid by their bosses. They sent 'em here. It's a collaboration."

The kid paused for a couple of seconds. "Mind if I watch?"

I thought he might have the idea that if he showed interest, someone might put him on after all.

Ainsworth gave his hard stare and shook his head. "We don't need gawkers hangin' around and gettin' hurt. You can watch from across the street." Then, in his usual manner, as if to cut off any further talk, he walked away.

Dunbar set down his end of the heavy post, and I did the same. Dunbar said, "What's your name?"

"Ed."

"Goin' to Montana, eh? What part?"

"Helena. But I want to go through Thermopolis on the way. See the Hot Springs."

"Well, I hope you make it. Here's this, to help you stay out of trouble." Dunbar had taken off his gloves and now handed the kid a silver dollar.

Time seemed to stand still for a couple of seconds. The kid had an uncertain look on his face, perhaps a combination of disbelief and humility. He blinked his eyes a couple of times, brightened, and said, "Thanks, mister. I'll remember you." He

104

shook Dunbar's hand, then mine, though I hadn't taken off my gloves, and he went on his way.

I was trudging from the lumber pile, by myself, carrying two planks for cross-members, when Dick Ainsworth stepped in front of me and blocked my way. Up close, I could see the thickening around his head and neck and the creases on his face.

"What-all did you tell that tramp of a kid?"

"Nothing."

"I heard you mention the boss's name."

"That was all."

"I heard you say he wasn't around much."

"I think I said that I didn't see him very much."

"Same thing." Ainsworth stepped closer, and a small spray of saliva flew out as he spoke. "Listen to me. You got no call talkin' to strangers about the boss. You got that? And I don't want to see you standin' around lolly-gaggin' when you should be workin'."

"I was just—"

"Don't talk back to me, or I'll make your head spin. You understand?"

"Yes, sir." All this time, I had been holding the two heavy planks. My main thought as he walked away was that I didn't think he dared talk that way to Dunbar.

I caught drifts of talk as I offered biscuits and poured coffee at noon dinner. Word had gotten around that a stranger had been looking for work and was turned away.

Borden Crowley had shown up for the meal and was seated on a three-legged camp stool. Mullet, Larose, and Ainsworth sat on the ground in a semicircle facing him.

Mullet said, "Next chance you git, I hope you hire one of

those drifters. Put him to work movin' the trash pile."

At the southeast corner of the shipping pen area, people in town had thrown bottles, cans, twists of wire, useless pots and pans, old shoes, and general refuse for a period of years. For the past few days, after hearing comments from some of the other workmen, I had wondered who was going to have the task of moving it. My fear, or dread, that Ainsworth would give me the job was becoming stronger.

Crowley gazed off in the direction of the rubbish heap, where the sunlight glittered on castaway whiskey bottles. "Not a bad idea," he said. "Some vagabond would be glad to have a job like that."

Mullet smiled and nodded at Larose.

Ainsworth spoke to the boss in a businesslike tone. "There's money for it, then?"

"Oh, yeah. We've got money for expenses. Everyone put up to begin with, or we couldn't have a stick of lumber here. The next tramp that comes along, put him on."

At dusk that evening, as if in answer to the wishes of Mullet, myself, and no doubt others, a stranger walked into our camp. I do not know that he would have looked better in broad daylight. He did not wear a hat or cap. He had tousled dark brown hair and an unkempt beard. He wore a collarless, two-button work shirt, grimy work jeans, and broken-down shoes. As he came up to the firelight, I saw that he had dark brown eyes, somewhat glazed, with yellow whites. Over his shoulder, he had slung an untidy bedroll tied with quarter-inch hemp twine. His eyes drifted around the fire as he ran the tip of his tongue across his lips. When he spoke, his voice came out rough.

"Someone said you might have work."

Dick Ainsworth fixed his gaze from where he sat on the ground. "Big boss isn't here, but you can talk to me. Where'd you come from?"

"Traveled from the country up north on down to Ashton, then over here."

Ainsworth looked him up and down. "I hope you're not afraid of hard work."

"Not at all." As the man spoke, I saw that he had yellow teeth, with a few missing.

"Well, when you work under me, you don't pick your job."

"Natcherly."

"You can start in the morning. Get a good night's rest. Find a place to roll out your bed. By the way, what's your name?"

"Hodel. George Hodel."

"We already got one George here. You'll go by Hodel."

"It's my name." He glanced around at the men who had plates in their laps. "Any chance of gettin' a bite to eat?"

"Sure. The kid there'll fix you up."

When the man stood close with his plate, I saw the broken veins on his face and smelled whiskey on his breath. I never begrudged a man a meal, and furthermore, I reminded myself that every man had to make his way through life, even if some men didn't have the best way of doing it.

I had to shake the hell out of Hodel to wake him in the morning, even though camp was milling all around. He had eaten three plates of beef and beans the night before, and I supposed he was making up for missed meals and lost sleep, not to mention sleeping off any prolonged effects of whiskey.

All he had for breakfast was biscuits, which he worked around in his mouth, and coffee, which he drank one cup after another until Ainsworth told him it was time to go to work.

With the old wheelbarrow, a pitchfork, and a square-nosed shovel, he undertook the rubbish pile. I had some sympathy for him, and I wasn't sure that I wouldn't be joining him at some point, anyway, so I kept an eye on him from time to time. By midmorning his face was shining with sweat. I wished I had a hat to lend him, but I didn't. He labored on, taking a trip to the water keg every half hour, and when he came to eat at midday, his face was flushed and his shirt was soaked with sweat.

Mullet seemed to feel sorry for him as well. "How are you getting along?" he asked.

"Nothin' to complain about."

"I know what you mean. Doesn't ever do me any good."

Hodel put on a feed as he had done the night before and drank about a half-gallon of water. Without a word, he crawled under the shade of the wagon and went to sleep.

When it was time to go back to work, Ainsworth told me to wake up the new fellow. I crawled under the wagon and gave Hodel a shake. He awoke with a start, wide-eyed.

"What?" he said.

"Dinner time's over. Back to work."

Hodel looked around him and said, "Oh. That's it."

He worked through the first three hours of the afternoon, though he seemed to pick and stab at the rubbish pile with less energy, and he made several trips to the water keg. Then, at about four o'clock, I lost track of him.

Ainsworth disappeared for a period of time as well, but I do not think they went to the same place. When they both showed up at suppertime, they did not pay any attention to one another. I guessed that Hodel had seen Ainsworth slip away and then did the same himself, but I told myself it didn't matter. For my part, I hoped Hodel didn't get fired before he moved all the trash.

I was minding the platters of fried beef as the men passed by and served themselves. Ainsworth ignored me and, it seemed to me, held his breath when he was near me. Hodel kept to himself at the end of the line, but when he came to where I stood, he looked at me with a relaxed expression and smiled.

"This is the best part of the day," he said.

I could have smelled the beer on his breath from a yard away. "Always a good time for me," I answered.

"I'll tell you, I thought stacking hay in the loft of a barn was the hottest, sweatiest work I ever did. And it might be. But today was a real hugger-mugger."

I interpreted him to mean it was a muggy day, so I said, "I do believe the humidity builds up a little in the latter part of the summer, on some days at least."

He winced as he shook his head. "Oh, the heat reflects off all them bottles and cans. Made the sweat just pour out of me."

"I know what you mean. It glances off this corral lumber more than a fella would think, too."

He relaxed his eyes on me. They seemed more glazed than before. "You know what I mean. That's more than some of these other sons of bitches care to do."

I forced a brief smile, and he moved on.

I wished he had taken a seat apart from the others, as he had done before, but I thought the beer might have made him more sociable. I was sure it made him talkative. He sat near the BC group of Mullet, Larose, and Ainsworth. At least Crowley himself had not joined the crew for supper. I would have cringed more if the big boss had been seated on his camp stool.

Ainsworth shifted to give a shoulder to Hodel, but the movement did not seem to have much effect.

Hodel's voice was gravelly when he raised it. "This is quite a town you've got here," he said.

The silence seemed to go down the ladder until Mullet said, "We get along."

"So I heard."

Ainsworth flared his nostrils and rubbed his finger across the bottom of his nose.

Hodel spoke again as he chewed a piece of meat back and forth with the teeth he had. "Some kind of town. You've got a poor working man killed, and no one does a thing about it."

"Not sure what you mean," said Mullet.

"I heard his name was Pearson."

"Oh, that. It's been reported to the law, and I b'lieve they're workin' on it."

"Not much, from what I heard."

Larose set his knife on his plate with a clack. "Sounds like you might've drunk too much pissy whiskey when you disappeared this afternoon."

Ainsworth's eyebrows went up, and the hard look came to his face. "Is that right?"

"You don't like what you hear." Hodel wagged his head as he looked down to cut another piece of meat.

Ainsworth shifted so that he could level his gaze on Hodel. "I don't like a man slippin' away and drinkin' on the job."

"Hah. Look who's talkin'. I saw where you went."

"I had a meeting. I wasn't sneakin' away. No wonder someone like you can't hold down a job."

Hodel didn't answer as he went back to his meal. I wondered if he was trying not to get fired or if he was thinking of what to say next. Either way, I felt a relief at the moment. The other men resumed eating, and I saw a chance to serve a plate for myself.

Mullet finished his meal and pushed himself to his feet. He carried his plate and utensils to the wreck pan and tossed them in. On his way back to his group, he paused next to Hodel. In a good-natured tone he said, "I heard you tell the kid you had a job stackin' hay. Where was that?"

"Up on Old Woman Creek. That's north of here, on the way to Newcastle."

"I know where it is."

Hodel did not look up from cutting a bite of beef.

Mullet, still lingering, said, "Did you work the whole season?"

"Two days of that is season enough for me."

I was forming a picture of that area myself, east of Lance Creek, which Del Bancroft had mentioned, and south of the Cheyenne River, when movement at the edge of the camp drew my attention. Borden Crowley, dressed in a hat and suit of dull silverish-gray, walked into the firelight.

He cleared his throat and said, "I hope it's not too late for whatever's in the pot."

"Not at all," said Dan as he rose from the box he was sitting on. "Eat your supper, Bard. I'll tend to him."

Mullet walked out of the light and headed toward the BC wagon. A minute later, he returned with the three-legged stool with a leather seat. He put it in place, and when the boss was settled, Dan brought him a plate of fried beef and potatoes.

Crowley cut at a piece of meat. "Everything all right? No problems?"

"Nothing to speak of," said Ainsworth.

Hodel had his elbows out as he cut his last piece of beef. He took in a long, sniffing breath, cleared his throat, and said, "Oh, we had things to speak of."

Crowley flicked a glance. "You're the new man, aren't you?"

"That's right. Name's Hodel."

The boss did not answer.

"In charge of the trash heap." Hodel cleared his throat again. "We were talking about what kind of a town this is."

"Not a big item for conversation, I'd think."

Hodel did not take what I was sure was a hint. He spoke again in his rough voice. "We were talking about a man who was killed, and how people don't seem to care to do anything about it."

"I believe it's in the hands of the law."

"I heard that. And I also heard this place has a reputation for lettin' men get away with things of that sort."

Crowley paused with his knife and fork. "You speak in the plural. Do you think one incident gives you the right to speak as if it was a trend?"

"Hah. Maybe you weren't around when they hung the horse trader. From what I hear, it happened fifteen years ago, and that story hasn't gone away."

"You speak as if you know something about it. If you did, you'd know they didn't hang him. That was just a rumor. Shows you how people talk when they don't know."

Hodel chewed as he spoke. "Don't be so sure there's not someone who does know. For every man that gets shot in the back or lynched, there might be someone hidin' in the brush gettin' a look at the ones that done it. Like up in Johnson County, just for an example. A smart person keeps his mouth shut, but sooner or later, someone's likely to hear a peep."

Crowley had not yet taken a bite. He sat in a slumped and brooding posture as he took in a long breath and exhaled. I was surprised to hear him speak this much, and I was surprised to see him give his full attention to Hodel.

"You sound as if you've heard a few stories yourself."

Hodel gave a wide-eyed, glassy stare. "I'd bet I've heard as many as you and your little foreman put together."

I could see Ainsworth bristle, but he kept still and said nothing.

Crowley raised his chin as he looked down on the man. "It seems to me you've had something to drink. Maybe you should go back to that."

"Not yet. I need to earn another day's pay."

Crowley handed his plate to Larose and pushed himself up from his seat. "Not here." Taller than average when others were standing, he loomed above the company as he took self-assured steps toward Hodel. He reached into his pocket, took out a silver dollar, and dropped it onto the man's plate. "That's for your day's work. Now get out."

After Hodel had rolled his blankets and Crowley had eaten his grub and gone, some of the hands muttered about a man getting fired for speaking his mind. Others said it was for drinking on the job.

Ainsworth raised his voice and said, "You might as well argue about the chicken and the egg. If he hadn't got drunk, he wouldn't have shot off his mouth. But he wouldn't have done either if he wasn't the type of man he is. Just low class, that's all."

Dunbar joined me at the tailgate to help with the dishes. In a low voice, he said, "Too bad the chap couldn't make another day's wages, but I'm afraid he's the type that burns his bridges as he goes along."

"Where do you think he is now?"

"I'd guess he's in a saloon, maundering in his cups. I'd like to say I wish he had better sense, but I don't know what else you could expect. And as for going there on any single occasion, I've been in those places myself. So I try not to throw stones."

Chapter Eight

As I stood at the bar in The Missouri Primrose and gazed at the painting of the lady lying on the couch, I was surprised to see a detail I had not remembered. In addition to lounging on one elbow with her tawny tresses covering some parts of her upper body and a gossamer scarf draped over her hip and waist area, she held a white flower dangling from her free hand. Now that I saw the flower and registered it, I realized I had seen the original many times, quite often on hillsides, in that cloudy, moist time of year that passes for spring in Wyoming.

Other than the flower, which had been easy to forget, nothing in the painting suggested a specific time or place. Like other paintings I have seen since then, it was raised in a lofty never-never land, above the hanging cloud of tobacco smoke, above the jingle of spurs, the clomp of boots, the chatter of voices, and the occasional slap of a leather dice cup.

The Saturday night crowd consisted of men from our building crew, working men from town, and ranch hands who rode in from the country. The atmosphere, as I felt it, had a general tone of relaxation, freedom from care or worry. Later on, men might whoop and holler in exuberance or raise their voices in anger, but the night was young. It seemed innocent and honest, a time to "drive dull cares away," as the song went. Beneath the surface, however, a memory nagged at me. I recalled George Hodel from the night before, tossing out remarks about malice and injustice for the benefit of anyone who would listen. I hoped and hoped he would not walk through the door tonight.

I drank from my glass of beer, mindful not to gulp it down too fast. It had a good taste after a week of sun and dust—and antagonism, I admitted. The ill will had worn on me, and I was glad to be away from it for a while.

Dunbar and Del Bancroft had fallen into a conversation next to me. I do believe they could have talked about building a wooden ark or a palace of ice. Second in rank to my fear that George Hodel might show up was a worry that someone would see me standing by myself and would try to engage me in a conversation. I would rather be left alone, to think about Emma or to brood about Dick Ainsworth and Boots Larose and the question of whether Alex Garrison ever stole a horse.

After half an hour of rumination and most of my glass of beer, I saw a full glass set in front of me.

"This man," said the bartender, pointing at Del Bancroft.

"Thank you," I said.

"You bet." Del smiled as he scratched his full head of hair. During the week he had worn a cloth cap, which I thought would be better than a hat when a man was working close to lumber, but he did not wear it to the saloon. I thought he seemed at ease, perhaps detached from the friction that was so evident between Crowley's men and Dunbar and myself.

Del went back to his conversation with Dunbar, and I realized I had been hearing someone tune a fiddle. Now the tentative notes of another instrument sounded. Looking around, past the tables and up against the opposite wall, I saw two musicians getting ready to play.

The fiddle player was tall and lean and gray-haired with a drooping mustache. The mandolin player was of medium height, light-haired, and clean-shaven. They looked as if they could have come from Ohio or Illinois, as they wore white shirts, brown vests and neckties, and brown derby hats. The word "minstrels" came to my mind.

They started off with a lively tune that identified itself as "Little Brown Jug." Before long, half the patrons were singing along. Next in the musicians' delivery was "The Little Old Log Cabin in the Lane," followed by "In the Baggage Coach Ahead," which I think I heard that evening for the first time but have heard many times since. After half a dozen numbers in this vein, including a couple of cowboy songs about lost love and heartache, it became apparent that this duo specialized in the sorrowful kind of music that was so popular. I had the illusion that these two men could be interchanged with any other pair who was playing that night in Chicago, Cincinnati, Pittsburgh, or Baltimore.

Then came an unexpected moment. The fiddle player held his bow as if to hold the audience's attention, and in a clear voice he said, "And now, if you don't mind, we'll play you something original. Mac and I wrote this song between us. It's called 'Traveler in the Snow,' and it goes like this."

With a light touch of the fiddle, blended with the clear, sad notes of the mandolin, they sang.

> *Well we found her one cold Sunday morning*
> *In the alley where hollyhocks grow.*
> *'Neath the dead leaves and husks of last summer's*
> *   stalks*
> *Lay the woman who died in the snow.*
>
> *She was wrapped in a coat and a blanket,*
> *But the night had gone twenty below.*
> *How she came to be there, to die all alone,*
> *Was something we never would know.*
>
> *For they come and they go on the train cars,*
> *And they drop off in towns like our own.*

They might stay for a day, and find nothing here,
Then they drift on to places unknown.

Oh, her face it was pale but not wrinkled,
Though her hair was beginning to gray.
And a necklace of gold, with a small garnet stone,
Cast a shine on a clear winter day.

For a moment, no more, she resembled
A person I'd known long ago.
Then the fancy passed on, and I saw as before
Just a woman who died in the snow.

Just a woman who died and was buried
At a stop on her journey alone.
Though we knew not her name, we laid her to rest
With her necklace and small garnet stone.

Oh, they come and they go on the train cars
And they drop off in towns like our own.
They might stay for a day, and find nothing here,
Then they drift on to places unknown.

I joined in the applause, and I saw that Del Bancroft and
Dunbar had been listening as well. Although the song fit right
in with the rest of the minstrels' repertoire of sad and wistful
tunes, it indeed offered something original that night in a town
that was but a speck in the Wyoming grassland.

As Dunbar and I walked back to camp later that evening, Del
Bancroft having taken leave earlier, I felt relaxed from the five
or six glasses of beer I had drunk, and I felt relieved that nothing had disrupted the tranquility of the evening. The melody of
a song ran through my mind, and I placed it.

117

I said, "You have an interest in songs. What did you think of the one they sang about the woman who died in the snow?"

"Oh, it was a maudlin piece all right, but not doing any harm. It's like a great many songs you'll hear in taverns and such places, cities and towns alike."

"That's what I thought."

"Sad and sentimental, but with good reason. Go to a graveyard, read fifty or a hundred gravestones, and see if you don't get to feeling a little sad yourself. Infants, young mothers—"

"But the woman in the song was gray."

"Oh, yes, but the larger idea is that there's a great deal of sadness in life, people dying at all ages, and these songs touch upon it in various ways."

"Well, I liked the song all right, but some of them take it too far, don't they?"

Dunbar laughed. "It's a matter of taste, I think. Something that's syrupy and sentimental to one person is profound and moving to another. And some people just like misery."

"For entertainment."

"Or indulgence. Not long ago I heard a song for the first time that was horrendous to me. And here were the others in the tavern, singing right along like believers."

"What was it called?"

"Something like 'A Picture from Life's Other Side.' That was in the refrain. Dreadful song. By comparison, it makes the song about the woman in the snow seem like stoic philosophy." After a few seconds he said, "Also, it was hard for me to drive the melody away. It was like 'Green Grow the Lilacs.' You hear someone sing that song, and you can't get the tune out of your head for days."

"That's the way it is with this song. I can still hear it."

"Now that you mention it, I can, too."

I awoke in the gray of morning inside the pyramid-shaped tent that Dunbar and I shared at the work camp. This Sunday being a day off, Dan did not sound the call before daybreak. As I lay in my blankets, I heard the muttering of voices from the direction of the campfire. I imagined Dunbar was out there, too, for he was not in the tent.

As I stepped out through the flap, I caught the smell of woodsmoke. Dan was mixing pancake batter in a large tin pan, and he had not lit a lantern. The camp had a subdued aura about it, as only three other men sat around the fire, and they kept their voices low.

I asked Dan if he had seen Dunbar, and he said he hadn't. I imagined Dunbar must have gotten up early and gone on some kind of an errand. I washed my face at the washbasin and asked Dan if he needed any help. He told me he could use me later, so I poured a cup of coffee and sat by myself near the fire.

Before long, Dan had hotcakes coming off the two cast-iron skillets. The day was brightening, and men came to the fireside in ones and twos. I had not yet decided what I was going to do for the day, so I kept to my own thoughts and ate pancakes as they came to me.

The sun rose higher while I washed dishes. Some of the workmen meandered toward town, and in a little while two of them came back with surprised expressions on their faces. They spoke in turns.

"They found a dead body in the alley behind the mercantile."

"It's that drunk that worked here. Hodel."

"The hell," said Dan. "Do they know how he died?"

"He's got no blood on him. Can't see where he's been shot or stabbed."

"They say he probably sweated too much and then drank too much to make up for it."

Dan frowned. "That was Friday when he sweated so much. And he left here with a bellyful of grub."

"It's what they say."

"They say a lot of things." Dan glanced around. "I wonder where Dunbar is. You didn't see him, did you?"

"Not at all."

For a moment I had a terrible feeling that Dunbar might have something to do with Hodel's dying, that I didn't know Dunbar at all. Then I told myself to be rational, not to make any assumptions until I had evidence.

I said, "I'll go look for him as soon as I finish with the dishes."

Dan rubbed his hands on his apron. "Go ahead. I'll finish these."

"I won't be long." I washed and rinsed the rest of the dishes, and Dan wiped them. When we were done, I dried my hands and took off.

The town didn't have many places for me to look, and even fewer on Sunday morning. I took a peek at the railroad station, which was locked up and empty. I crossed the street to the Phelps Hotel.

There I found Dunbar, freshly shaved, sitting across the breakfast table from Mrs. Deville. She looked quite pretty in a white blouse, embroidered brown jacket, and matching skirt. Her dark hair hung loose to her shoulders but was held in place above her forehead with a slender diadem. Her eyes sparkled as she smiled at me.

Dunbar turned and said, "What, ho, my friend. What brings you here? Have you had breakfast? You know Mrs. Deville, don't you?"

I almost felt impatient with him. "Yes, I do," I said. "And I had breakfast. I'm sorry to interrupt yours, but I came with some bad news."

The humor vanished from his face. "What is it?"

I glanced at Mrs. Deville.

Dunbar said, "If it's private—"

"Not so much, I don't think. Excuse me if it's out of place, but they found George Hodel in the alleyway. He's not alive anymore."

"That's bad." Dunbar picked up his napkin from his lap, then set it down. "I think I need a couple of minutes."

"I'll wait outside."

I left him there and went out to sit on the bench near the front door. A dozen thoughts ran through my mind. The idea of Hodel lying dead did not make sense. At least it did not sink in all at once. I was relieved to know that Dunbar was not connected. His reaction told me that much. Also, his being spruced up helped me understand where he had been. I guessed that he had gone to the hotel early, ordered a bath, and shaved himself while he was at it. In addition to all of this, I had the surprise of seeing that he knew Mrs. Deville. Thinking back, I realized what I had sensed right away when I saw them together—that they knew each other, that they had some level of confidentiality or intimacy. On its own, it seemed harmless, almost a good joke on Boots Larose and any wolves that needed to be kept at bay. In a broader context, the cozy scene jarred with my awareness of the unwashed George Hodel lying dead in the alley.

Dunbar stepped outside and put on his hat. "Which way?"

I motioned toward the west. "This way. They said he was in back of the mercantile."

We walked along the sidewalk with the morning sun slanting in on our left. I told Dunbar about the prevailing theory that Hodel had sweated too much and then drunk himself to death. Dunbar raised his eyebrows and sniffed.

We crossed the side street, walked past The Missouri

Primrose, and came to the mercantile. The door was locked.

"We should have gone around to the alley to begin with," I said.

We walked back the way we came, arrived at the corner, and turned left. Across the side street, The Bower appeared to be closed, which would be normal on Sunday morning.

We turned left at the alley. Up ahead, a small group had gathered at the back door of the mercantile. We walked past a stand of hollyhocks blooming dark pink at the top of the stalks, now in late summer. I recalled the song from the night before.

The back door of the mercantile was open, and a smaller group of people stood inside. We pushed our way through the crowd outside, excusing ourselves. I exchanged a wordless glance with Otto Trent and Carl Granger.

Inside the storeroom, as some people looked on with curiosity and others had reverent expressions on their faces, George Hodel lay on a table with his arms folded on his chest. He looked as I had seen him last, except his eyes were closed. I told myself again not to jump to conclusions, but I was quite convinced that he had not brought about his own death.

It's not fair, I thought.

"Who's taking care of him?" Dunbar asked.

A neatly dressed man whose name I did not remember said, "We brought him in here to get him out of the alley. The barber's out of town until tomorrow." The man gave Dunbar a close look. "You're not related, are you?"

"We knew him," said Dunbar. "He worked with us for a day on the corral project."

"That's what they say, that he worked there."

"Day before yesterday," Dunbar continued. "I wonder what he did for twenty-four hours or more."

The man raised his eyebrows. "I imagine he spent most of that time drinking up his wages."

"He had a dollar. At ten cents a glass, that's not enough to kill a man."

"I don't know. I've never tried to drink that much."

Dunbar cast a glance over the corpse and raised his eyes to the well-dressed man. "And you are—?"

The man raised his chin. "Matthew Fenster. I'm the proprietor here."

Dunbar surprised me by taking a friendly tack. "Well, it's a decent thing you're doing for this man."

"I don't know what else I could do."

"He's not able to thank you, so I'll say it on his behalf."

Fenster shrugged.

For no reason I can explain, except that I felt the need to say it, I said, "Every man has a life. Every person, really."

Fenster seemed relieved to be talking to me. "That's right, son. I think there's something like that in Corinthians."

The sun was climbing toward the high spot as we walked down the alley the way we came. When we arrived at the side street, I saw that the front door of The Bower was open. The head of a broom flicked out and then back into the shadow.

Dunbar motioned with his hand without pointing. "Now there's a person who might know something. Shall we drop in?"

"We're in no hurry otherwise," I said.

Mary Weldon appeared in the doorway as we walked across the street. She waited, broom in hand, until we reached the footpath in front of her establishment. She wore a white apron over a gray dress, and her light brown hair was pinned up.

"Good morning," she said. "I don't think it's past noon yet."

"How do you do?" Dunbar took off his hat, and I did the same.

"Well enough, considering," she said. "I suppose you've heard the news that's been running up and down the alley."

"We just came from there. Did you know the deceased?"

The woman did not show any emotion. "Not very much."

Dunbar made a slight wave with his hat in my direction. "We did. He worked with us for the better part of a day. We're working on the shipping pens, you know."

"He said he worked there."

Dunbar glanced toward the main street. "It's a bit awkward, standing out here and talking about this sort of thing."

"I'm not open for business right now."

Dunbar shrugged. "We weren't expecting to order a dram. Just exchange a few words, if there's some way we can do right by Mr. Hodel."

She relaxed her defenses. Glancing at the main street and then past us toward the alley, she said, "Come on in."

She closed the door behind us and led the way into the dark tavern. At the far end of the bar, she lit a lamp and took her position behind the polished surface. The place was quiet, and it gave me a funereal feeling to realize that I might be standing where the late patron downed his drink.

"Mr. Hodel was talkative," said Dunbar, in a low voice that sounded both respectful and cautious.

"That he was." The woman's bluish-gray eyes moved from Dunbar to me and back to him.

"I suppose if he was in here very long, he went on about a few things."

"He did. He was in here yesterday afternoon and evening, as well as a couple of hours the afternoon before. He had a capacity for drink."

Dunbar nodded. "And he seemed to have some favorite topics, at least in the short while that he visited with us."

Mary Weldon's eyebrows raised half an inch and relaxed.

"Perhaps he touched upon one or two of them in here."

The landlady tipped her head as if to say, "Perhaps," but she let Dunbar take the lead.

"He seemed fond of talking about a recent killing, and I don't know but what he might have come upon that topic in here."

"He might have. That first afternoon, there were a couple of other customers in here, and he took interest in their stories."

"And I imagine they might have mentioned an incident from several years back, about an old horse trader who was killed."

"Oh, yes. That story comes up now and again, and they chewed it over as well."

Dunbar drew a breath. "Mr. Hodel seemed to enjoy suggesting that there might have been witnesses to one crime or another."

Mary Weldon shook her head. "I don't remember that. People talk on and on in here, and I don't interrupt as long as it stays decent. I don't recall anyone talking about witnesses, but someone may have passed a remark. I don't know."

"I see. Well, there's no telling." Dunbar took me in with a glance and returned to the landlady. "I say, it must be past twelve by now."

"I believe it is."

"What would you think of a glass of refreshment for my young friend and me?"

She shrugged. "I usually don't open until a little later on Sunday, but there's no law against it. Same as before?"

"It was agreeable last time. And you, Bard?"

"Fine with me," I said.

The woman poured two tall glasses of beer and set them before us.

Dunbar laid a silver dollar on the counter. "For future indemnity."

She glanced at the coin but did not touch it. "You could be a lawyer."

"I'm a cowpuncher." Dunbar put his dark hat on his head

125

and set it back.

The woman gave a wry smile, and I thought I could feel her womanly presence a little more than when we first came in.

Dunbar took a sip of beer and set down his glass. "Just as good as before," he said.

Mary Weldon nodded.

"But you know we didn't come in here just to drink."

"I guessed that."

"Not to beat around the bush, but Bill Pearson's widow told me he used to come in here on occasions as well."

The lady winced. "If you mean there's a tendency for men who come in here to end up dead, I'll have to question it."

Dunbar shook his head. "Not at all. I'm interested in Bill Pearson by himself at the moment. He was a customer, wasn't he?"

She gave a mild shrug of concession. "He came in from time to time to have a dram, as you call it."

"An honest sort, I assume?"

"I never had a reason to think otherwise."

Dunbar touched his glass but did not take a drink. Meeting Mary Weldon's eyes, he said, "Bill's wife told us that he might have been worried on account of his having seen a man who had been in the neighborhood when Alex Garrison, the old horse trader, was killed."

"He may have been."

"Did he ever say anything to that effect when he was in here?" Dunbar took a drink.

"You mean gab with the other customers?" She shook her head.

"How about to you?"

The woman hesitated, as if she was uncertain how to answer. "Bill was an honest man, like you said. But he kept things close. If he ever said anything of that nature to me, it was confidential.

In my business, I hear of lot of things both public and private. I don't repeat things that men confide in me."

"Even if it's for a greater good?"

"That remains to be seen."

Dunbar nodded, as if in thought. After a moment he said, "I don't mean to be too forward. I'm sorry if I seem that way. I'll put things more clearly for the moment. When George Hodel was holding forth in our work camp about these two killings, he didn't come out and say that they had any connection. But it could have been taken that way."

"Well, I don't recall him putting things in those terms."

"And he wouldn't be led to make that connection by comments that he heard in here?"

"Not by anything I said, that's for certain. And I don't remember anyone else relating the two in the way that you mean." She folded her arms across her apron.

Dunbar took another drink. "It's too bad."

"In what way?"

"That we can't know more."

"I don't mean to be contrary, but people get punished for knowing too much."

"Or seeming to."

She tipped her head. "I've probably said more than I needed to already."

"It's safe with us," said Dunbar.

I felt that our conversation was nearing its end, so I took a full swallow of beer. I did not realize how dry my mouth had become, and the drink set well with me.

Mary Weldon took a short breath. "You seem to have a great deal of curiosity for a cowpuncher."

"I told Mrs. Pearson that if there was something I could do, I would do it."

The landlady held her pose with her arms folded. Her face

did not show much expression.

Dunbar finished his beer and set the empty glass on the bar. I took another drink from mine.

"I'd just as soon you not pay me for today," said the woman. "You overpaid me last time by quite a bit."

I thought she was regarding Dunbar's money as payment for sharing information, and I rather admired her for it.

Dunbar smiled. "The future indemnity I spoke of was for beer to take with us. Could we have three bottles?"

She gave a light frown. "Well, I suppose so. It's not cold."

"I'm sure we'll enjoy it."

"As you wish." From a lower cabinet in back of the bar she took out three dark bottles. From beneath the bar she took a length of brown paper that looked as if it had been used before, and she wrapped the three bottles as a merchant might wrap groceries for the saddlebags.

During this time, I finished my beer in two more drinks.

She handed the package to Dunbar and said, "I would appreciate it if you bring back the bottles."

"I will."

Outside, I squinted in the glare of the sun. We walked to the main street and turned left, then paused before crossing the street toward the work camp.

With no one close by, Dunbar said, "This thing that happened to Hodel is no good."

"Doesn't seem like it."

"You know, it's all good and fine to make light talk in our moments of leisure. Chat about maudlin songs, heroic deeds, ancient tragedies, and people falling into glaciers. You can be detached and philosophical, and you know you'll get back to business later. That's where we are now."

We stepped into the street and headed across. I observed Dunbar cradling the package wrapped in wrinkled brown paper as he gazed off in the distance. I recalled the image of George Hodel lying on the table, and my mind circled back to the question of why Dunbar had ordered three bottles of beer.

CHAPTER NINE

We found Del Bancroft sitting on the shady side of the wagon that held the hinges, bolts, and nails for the corrals. He was reading a book. When he saw us, he tucked in a small slip of paper to hold his place, closed the book, and raised his eyes to meet us.

As we drew close, I saw that he was reading the second volume of Grant's memoirs.

"What's new?" he asked.

Dunbar answered. "I ended up with three bottles of beer, and I thought you might like to join us."

"Do you have a place in mind?"

"What do you think of going over to the corrals and admiring our work?"

Del's brown eyes searched both of us. "Sure. Let me put this book away and put on a hat."

A minute later, he was ready to go. The three of us walked to the corrals, where we were out of earshot of the camp. We found a patch of shade where the floor planks of the first ten feet of the catwalk overhead had been nailed in place. We sat on the ground, and Dunbar uncapped the three bottles.

Del said, "This news about Hodel does not sound good."

"Not at all," said Dunbar. "And he seems to have fallen victim to the very thing he was railing about. No one seems inclined to look for answers."

"What do you think?"

"I don't want to put things in strong terms, and I don't want to make accusations, but I don't think he drank himself to death."

"I don't disagree, but how do you think he would have died?"

"There are ways that don't draw blood or leave bruises. Chloroform is common. And injection is becoming more so. Then there's good old-fashioned poison, which would have been harder to administer to him. It's favored by people who live under the same roof, though someone could slip it into a drink." Dunbar took a quick survey of the area around us. "It's easier to say what I don't think it was."

Del nodded and took a sip of beer. "I go along with your sense of caution, or maybe reluctance, in regards to saying things outright. A fellow needs proof."

"Oh, yes. No need to make accusations at this point. It's better to work on finding evidence." Dunbar tipped his bottle and took a swallow. "I have a hunch that these things—that is, what Hodel talked about and what happened to him—are related and that they go back to the death of Alex Garrison."

"Which in turn goes farther back to the question of why."

"Correct." Dunbar nodded. "And I think there's more to be known or brought out."

Del gave him a close look. "You mean you think there's a way of finding an answer about Alex."

"There might be. You know, he's buried out there somewhere. As I told Bard, he's been here all this time. If you believe in such things as the truth—that is, as something that has a life of its own, the answer has been here all this time as well."

"And you think there's a way of getting at it."

"I believe it exists, and I think it's worth a try. As I mentioned to the lady who runs the alehouse, I told Bill Pearson's wife I would do something if I could."

I thought Dunbar was waiting for some kind of indication

that Del Bancroft was with him.

Del said, "Somebody's got to do something. I'm not sure that I'm the one to do it, but I would give it my support."

"That's good to hear." Dunbar took another glance around. I did the same, and I saw no one. Dunbar lowered his voice. "So tell me. Did Alex Garrison have any friends back then? Anyone who's still around?"

Del pursed his lips. "Seems to me that he was friends with a woman named Rona. Not a romantic friendship. You'll know what I mean if you ever meet her. They were both—well, not outcasts or misfits, but just not part of what you might call society—to the extent that we have it here. They didn't fit in very well, but they had a kind of kinship between them. Every once in a blue moon, you'd see her on her way to his place or on the way back."

"Rona," said Dunbar. He turned to me. "Do you know her?"

"Not personally. I know who she is, and I think I know where to find her. The last I knew, she worked for Luke Hayward."

"That's right," said Del. "He's got quite a menagerie, and she tends to his animals. Feeds 'em, nurses bum calves, cleans pens, and such."

"How far out is it?"

Del looked at me. "A couple of hours, maybe more?"

I nodded and yawned. The beer was making me drowsy in the hot weather, and I did not relish the idea of going on a long ride.

Dunbar, meanwhile, seemed to have perked up. "Sounds good. What do you say, Bard? We'll play guessing games to keep you awake."

"Such as?"

"Who died first, John Adams or Thomas Jefferson?"

I said, "They died on the same day. The fiftieth anniversary of the signing of the Declaration of Independence."

"Yes, but who died first?"

"I don't know. I don't believe I ever learned it."

"Guess."

I heaved out a short breath. "I don't know. John Adams."

"That was what he thought. His final words were something like, 'Thomas Jefferson still lives,' but unbeknownst to him, Jefferson had died earlier in the day. Easy mistake. News didn't travel as fast in those days."

I said, "Well, it was a fair question, I suppose."

"And it was a true guessing game. Not like some of these riddles."

"Like the one about walking on four legs, two legs, and three legs."

Del said, "Oh, yes. I remember that one. We learned it somewhere along the way."

"Like geometry," said Dunbar. "Here's another one. And I'll promise not to plague you with any more. What is it that no man wants to have, but no man wants to lose?"

"I don't know. There are too many possibilities. This is a riddle, isn't it?"

"Yes. Shall I tell you the answer?"

"Go ahead. Get it over with."

"Said with true irony. A bald head."

I thought, that was a safe joke. Everyone present had a full head of hair.

Del said, "You've got a regular supply of gallows humor."

Dunbar tipped the neck of his beer bottle as he gave a mild shrug. "Or guillotine."

As Dunbar and I rode away from the work camp, I cast a glance backward. Seeing the main gateway with its crossbeam, plus the catwalk to the right, I had a momentary vision in which I put the two parts together. They made a scaffold or gallows. I had

133

never seen such a structure in person, but I had seen illustrations, including one that showed the four conspirators being hanged for the Lincoln assassination conspiracy.

We stopped long enough for Dunbar to skip into the alehouse and return the empty bottles. Between the hot sun and the beer I had drunk, I was feeling drowsy. I shook my head and focused on the ride that lay before us. Luke Hayward's place lay south and west of town in an area where the grassland was a little poorer and the Niobrara wasn't much more than a muddy trickle.

Dunbar was whistling a tune. After a few bars, I recognized it as the song about the woman who died in the snow. At some point he quit whistling, but I didn't notice, because the tune was running through my head as well.

I led us west out of town about five miles until we came to a trail leading south. We turned left and followed the trail through rolling country.

A couple of miles later, Dunbar said, "Let's ride for that high spot over there." He pointed to the left.

When we gained the high ground, we had a good lookout for several miles in each direction. I said, "What do you have in mind?"

He had his brows drawn together as he studied the country. "I want to see if we're being followed. If we're going to talk to someone who might know something, I don't want to be giving away a witness."

"A good thought." I let my gaze wander across the landscape, and I felt the atmosphere pressing on me. The air was still, and the summer heat lay like a blanket upon the land. Here where the grass was sparse, the soil absorbed and reflected the rays of the sun. A man standing on the ground could feel it through his boots, and I wondered if the horses felt it in their hooves.

"Big country," said Dunbar. "You'd think there was enough

room for everyone. But no matter how far people are spread apart, there's always someone who has to encroach on others. He's not happy under his own vine and fig tree. He's got to pester and meddle, or covet, or antagonize, or violate someone else's health and happiness."

"It's a bad part of human nature," I said.

"That's it. It's a constant part, not just a strange occurrence or an occasional exception. You can go a thousand miles in any direction under Heaven's dome, and they're scattered everywhere. Maybe at wide intervals, but they're out there, devising pain and suffering and death because they're not happy with what they've got. It's perverse. Sometimes it's as if they want others to suffer because they themselves are miserable."

"Do you think they choose to be that way?"

"It's hard to say. In some way, people don't choose the way they are. Old bachelors for example, or men who can't keep their hands to themselves. But they can choose how to act or behave." Dunbar peered at me in a sidelong way. "Are you trying to nail me down on the subject of free will? I should never have talked about the Presbyterians and the Methodists."

"It's just something to think about."

"Oh, yes. Predestination and free will. I suppose we all have to think about it sooner or later. When it comes to deep ideas, though, I'm more of a cowpuncher than a philosopher. And when I do indulge, I don't tie hard and fast to a single theory. For example, our friend Hodel. I wouldn't say he was that way because he wanted to be, and I wouldn't say he couldn't help it. For me, it's a combination. It's the way he was."

Still scanning the country, I said, "Well, however he was, including a bit offensive, I don't think he deserved to die the way we think he did. That is, if he did."

"Especially the 'if' part."

"No assumptions."

"Not hard and fast. Just hypothesis. At this point, at least."

We rode into Luke Hayward's place in the late afternoon when the shadows were growing longer. I took in the barnyard with a broad sweep, noting pens that held milk cows, calves, hogs, sheep, and goats. Chickens and geese wandered loose. And on the peak of a shed, a peacock perched, with its long tail reaching to the eaves. For as long as I had known of the woman referred to as Rona, I understood that she lived and worked there. I knew her only by sight, and I had not seen her for a year or two. But when the door of a weathered shed opened and a bulky figure walked out, I recognized her.

She had the heavy build of a woman in later middle age, and she was dressed in loose-fitting men's clothes. She wore tall, common boots, too thick for riding, with her trousers legs tucked in—the better to avoid manure and spatter, I imagined. She walked at an uneven gait, using her stock-tending stick as a walking stick as well. In her free hand she carried a feed bucket.

I waved to her and swung down from my horse. Dunbar dismounted as well. Rona set down the feed bucket and walked toward us.

She came to a stop a couple of yards away. She was wearing a canvas cap with a short, wide bill. I noticed her hacked gray hair, clouded face, and full, round nose. When she spoke, I saw yellow teeth with a gap on the lower row.

"Afternoon. Are you lookin' for someone?"

I said, "We were hoping to find a woman named Rona. Is that you?"

"I answer to that. My original name is Verona, but people shorten it."

"Well, my name's Bard Montgomery, and this is my work partner, Mr. Dunbar. We work for Lou Foster."

Her eyes went to Dunbar and back to me. "Good to meet you," she said. She took out a bag of Bull Durham from her trousers and began to roll a cigarette.

"Likewise," said Dunbar, unhurried. "We hope not to interfere with your work."

"I figger you come for somethin'."

"We did. You know, there have been some suspicious things going on."

She nodded without looking up.

"And to some of us, at least, they seem to go back to Alex Garrison."

Verona's eyes narrowed as she studied her work. "I don't know how much good it does to talk about any of that."

"I know what you mean. People get hurt, or worse, for seeming to know too much and for talking about it."

"Either or both. So that's why I don't talk much. About that kind of thing, anyway."

Dunbar waited for her to meet his eyes. "I don't know if you've heard the most recent—"

"If you mean Bill Pearson, I have."

"I meant something more recent than that. Just last night, a fellow named George Hodel died. He had drifted into town, stayed a couple of days. He worked where we were building corrals. Worked hard, but he had a tendency to drink and then talk. He got wind of the Bill Pearson story and the Alex Garrison story, and he made a public case about how no one does anything about these killings."

Verona licked the seam and tapped it. "Not much sense in that. Talk that way."

"You're right. They found him dead in the alley. This morning."

Verona stopped with the cigarette halfway to her mouth. "Just like that?"

"Well, he wasn't like the others, because they didn't find a bullet hole or bruises or stab wounds or anything."

She let out a tired breath and made ready to light her cigarette.

"So here's how I see it," said Dunbar. "If a person knows something and holds it back, he makes it easier for the bad ones to get away with it."

Verona had a troubled expression on her face as she looked down her nose, struck a match, and held the flame to the end of her cigarette. "I know what you mean." She puffed, and a cloud of smoke rose in front of her face. "I'll tell you this much. Alex and I were friends, nothing more. I went to see him every now and then. Often as not, it was about a horse. I lived on my own at the time. We talked about other things, never anything big. Just more than business, that was all, and I might hang around for an hour or two. Just gabbin', really."

"Normal enough."

"Seemed like it."

"I would say you knew him better than many others did."

"Maybe so. But my point is, I knew him well enough to stick around and chat. And that's how I happened to be there one time when something happened."

"Oh," said Dunbar, in a tone that invited her to go on.

I thought she was still unsure about how much to tell, for she wrinkled her nose and stared at her cigarette. Then she spoke.

"It's one of those things that you don't ask for, and it doesn't make any sense, but you get drawn into it. Or Alex did, anyway, because it happened at his place." She hesitated again. "But like I say, I don't know how much good it does to talk about it. I don't think Alex mentioned it to anyone, and look how he ended up."

"What do you think he would want?"

"Oh, at this point?" She turned to me. "Excuse my language,

but I think he would say don't let the sons of bitches get away with it."

Dunbar said, "From what I know of him, I think you're right."

She narrowed her eyes on him. "What stake do you have in this, then?"

"I told Bill Pearson's wife I would do something if I could. Beyond that, I don't like to see people get away with crooked and dirty things."

She puffed a couple of times on her cigarette, as if it was a pipe, then let out a long, slow breath without smoke. "Well, all right. It was like this. I was visiting Alex one time, talking about trading a horse, when a kid showed up." Her lips flattened out on the stub of her cigarette, and she took a drag to inhale.

"Traveling?"

"On foot. And scared to hell. Alex gave him something to eat, and the kid blubbered out a story." Verona shook her head. "I've thought about it a thousand times, and it's always the same. Bad. Just bad."

It seemed to me that she kept stopping short but knew she should follow through. I said, "And both you and Alex heard it?"

"Yes." She took a breath. "It went like this. The kid was workin' at a sheepherding camp up on Old Woman Creek. North of the Hat Creek Breaks. I don't know where for sure. That creek flows for a long ways as you go up the trail."

"Sure," said Dunbar.

"Anyway, the kid was the camp tender, and there was one sheepherder. The way the kid told it, one night an overbearing kind of man came into their camp. A stranger, and he was on horseback. He rode up close to their fire. The sheepherder asked what he wanted, and the man said that he wanted them to get the hell out of the country, that he hated sheep, and he'd brought along a club to kill a thousand of 'em. The kid said he went on threatening like that, and the kid wondered if he was tryin' to work himself up to it. The man's voice got shaky, and the sheepherder laughed at him. He said he didn't think the man had the nerve to kill any sheep. That did it. The stranger flew into a fit. He piled off his horse, grabbed hold of the sheepherder, and clubbed him to death. The kid tried to stop him, but the stranger threw him aside. The kid tried to pull himself together, but he was half-paralyzed with fear and he didn't know what to do. He tried to run. The stranger chased him down, grabbed him by the shirt, and dragged him back to the fire." Verona took a drag on her cigarette. "The kid said he thought the man had run out of energy, or had lost his nerve again, or somethin' like that. The kid looked him in the eye, and the man couldn't take it. That was what the kid said. He gave the man a look that said, I know what you are and I saw what you did. The man let him loose."

I nodded to her to go on.

"The kid said the man's voice was shaking again, but he still lorded it over him. He told the kid that if he didn't leave the country for good, never come back, he would have him hunted down and killed in a way that no one would think a thing of it. So the kid ran while he had a chance. He thought that as soon as the stranger got his nerve together again, he *would* send someone after him."

Dunbar said, "Did this kid ever say what the stranger looked like?"

"Oh, yes, and I remember. He said the man was tall and well dressed, not some range rider. He had light-colored hair and was clean-shaven."

"That's not much, but it's something."

Verona stuck out her lower lip. "It reminded Alex and me of someone we knew, but like you say, it wasn't a very full description, and this kid wasn't going to stick around."

Dunbar said, "He was lucky, in one way, at least. Some witnesses get run out of the country, like he did, but others don't make it that far. They just disappear."

"Well, he got away all right, as far as I know. He took off across country in the dark."

"And Alex?"

"Oh, he never peeped. But the fellow we were reminded of started acting fishy, as if he knew the kid had stopped there at Alex's place."

"What about the kid? What did he look like?"

Verona pushed out her lips and made a small frown. "There wasn't much to him. Thin and not very tall. He had straight blondish hair and blue eyes."

Dunbar nodded in a way that I thought I recognized, somewhat routine, as if he didn't have much interest. But I had the impression that he had heard some of this story before.

He drew his brows together. "Why did you never come forward about this?"

"Puh. Like I said earlier, you figger there's more harm than good that can come out of it. First off, I never had any proof. Second, Alex was dead, and I couldn't change that. If he did get killed for having stolen horses, which I doubted but couldn't say for certain, I didn't want to be a part of it. And if he was killed for knowing something—well, I didn't want anyone to know that I had some of the same knowledge."

"So you've never told this story to anybody."

"No, sir. And I wouldn't have told you if I didn't trust you. And this kid, too."

"But to go all this time and not tell anyone. Two men were killed."

She rubbed her nose. "I've always felt sorry for that. But I did what I thought I had to. As for the first man who was killed, I only knew what I had heard. I didn't see it, and I didn't know for sure who the stranger was. I don't spread stories I'm not sure of. You don't know what might come back. My life wouldn't be worth much to some people." She shifted her eyes, twisted her mouth, then came back to look at both of us. "It's not just that I don't have a nickel to my name." She took a breath, as if she was still uncertain about what to say. "I was never a pretty girl. I never cared about men. I didn't choose to be that way. I just was. But a lot of people don't care much about you or what happens to you when you're not like them."

Dunbar nodded. "Well, it's good that you're telling us now."

"Maybe I'm soft. Like I said, I trust you." Her eyes were like small, gray, cloudy agate marbles as she turned them to me. "And this boy. Maybe he reminds me of that other kid." She blinked. "I felt sorry for him. More than sorry." Her cigarette had gone out. She turned it in her fingertips, dropped it, and stepped on it with her coarse boot. She took a breath as she stood with her head lowered. "The whole thing made no sense, and it's probably still a nightmare to him." She looked up from the ground. "The main reason I'm telling someone now is like you said. If you don't say something, you're helping the person who did the wrong. And I don't think it's over."

"I'm afraid you might be right."

"This has all come back to haunt me since I heard about Bill Pearson. The way I see it, you've got a sheepherder, a horse trader, and a dirt-grubber, all killed."

"And maybe a traveling drunk."

"I don't know about him, except what you said. But with these others, I don't think someone should get away with doing in someone else just because he's low and poor and got no one to do anything about it."

"I'm glad you've seen a reason to tell what you know."

She shrugged. "It could put me next on the list, but I guess that's a chance I've got to take." She leveled her cloudy agate eyes on Dunbar. "I don't think I need to tell you to be careful about who you talk to or what you tell 'em." She pointed at me with her thumb. "And I hope this young fellow understands."

The sun was slipping in the west, and any drowsiness I had felt earlier in the day had vanished. The seriousness of the situation seemed very clear to me.

"Don't worry about him," said Dunbar. "He understands."

I felt that I should be able to speak for myself, but I also felt that no more needed to be said on this topic. I nodded to her and said, "Thanks for telling us what you know."

We left her to do her chores, and after watering our horses, we mounted up and rode out of the yard. Behind us, the sheep and the goats and the calves made a ground-level chorus as the peacock on the roof sent out its long, strange, choking call. It ran a chill through my neck and shoulders.

Dusk was drawing in as we rode toward town. We rode through a muddy draw, following the trail through a marshy area with cattails, and I realized we had crossed the Niobrara.

A little while later, up on the warm, dry grassland again, Dunbar took to whistling the tune to the song about the woman who died in the snow. I thought it sounded like a song of celebration in comparison with what we had heard at Luke Hayward's.

CHAPTER TEN

A scarlet sunrise was giving way to an orange and yellow sky when Dick Ainsworth stopped to loom over Dunbar and me. We were sitting on the ground between the campfire and the chuck wagon, drinking coffee after a breakfast of bacon and fried potatoes. I had been thinking about our visit with Verona the day before, and I was imagining that the peacock was sending out its strange, piercing call with the sunrise.

"You two," said Ainsworth, with a brief pause, "can finish the job of moving the trash pile. We need it out of the way so we can build the corner there."

Dunbar looked up and seemed to be studying the man.

"Any questions?" asked Ainsworth. His dusty black hat cast his face in shadow as he bore down on us.

Dunbar shook his head. "Not from me."

"Me, either," I said.

"You know where the tools are." Ainsworth pivoted and turned his back on us.

As I finished my coffee, I mulled over this small turn in events. Ever since Hodel left, I was expecting to have the miserable job dumped on me, but I didn't expect Ainsworth to pull Dunbar away from Del Bancroft. If I had a good thought at all, it was in knowing that the work would go faster with two people.

We gathered our tools and took up where Hodel had left off. Dunbar never complained about the work that came his way, and he often had a cheerful air as he went about menial tasks, as if to say that he was never too good for that kind of work. But on this morning, he did not whistle or move about in a sprightly fashion. He worked almost with a vengeance, stabbing at the rubbish with a pitchfork and pushing the wheelbarrow with full force. I exerted myself as well, thinking we had best make as much progress as we could before the heat of the day came around.

The work itself was difficult and aggravating—disentangling wire and cloth from pieces of old furniture, rusted stovepipe, and an endless quantity of empty cans and bottles. All of it was cast-off debris that people threw out with the assumption that they would never see it again. And here we were, moving it to another heap, where perhaps someone else, years later, would have to deal with it again.

In the middle of the morning, after moving a couple of dozen wheelbarrow loads, we took a break and went to the wagon for a drink of water. I had the clean sensation of sweating from honest work, and I wiped at my face with my shirtsleeve.

As Dunbar and I drank from tin cups and crouched in the thin shade of the wagon, Dan covered the dough he was mixing and joined us.

"Looks like you boys got the dirty work."

In a matter-of-fact tone, Dunbar said, "Somebody has to do it. It's work."

"You wonder if Ainsworth is tryin' to get even for what you did to Larose, or whether he's got some other grudge."

"Don't know what it would be."

"Maybe not a grudge as much as a resentment. A kind of jealousy. Wants to keep everyone else below him, make sure no one rises. As if he felt someone was goin' to question his authority."

"It's more than I care to worry about," said Dunbar. "There's other things that at least I think are more serious."

Dan nodded.

Dunbar wet his lips after taking a drink of water. "This may or may not be related, but do you have any memory of a story about a sheepherder being killed up on Old Woman Creek? I'm guessing it would be about fifteen years ago."

Dan's pale blue eyes widened. "Oh, yeah. Bludgeoned. They thought his partner did it, because he disappeared."

"Huh. No one had any other theories?"

"Not that I recall. It seemed like one of those strange things that happen when people live off by themselves—alone, or in close company—and lose their bearings."

Dunbar said, "I've heard some of those stories. Sheepherders or prospectors all alone, or two men who get stuck in a cabin for the winter. That sort of thing."

"Is there somethin' that's got you interested in this story?"

"Well, any story is interesting when someone gets bludgeoned, shot, stabbed, or poisoned. But I would guess you mean whether it has a relation to other incidents."

Dan twisted his mouth. "Somethin' like that."

"Let's just say I'm working on that idea."

"Sure."

"And it would be all right if you didn't go out of your way to repeat a question I might have had."

Dan held his eyes on Dunbar. "Not with the things that have happened recently."

Dunbar and I worked through the rest of the morning. When we heard the triangle ringing at noon, we finished the wheelbarrow load we were working on and headed for the wagon. Several of the other hands had already served their grub and were seated on the ground. As I washed up, I heard a bit of chatter going around.

Dan told me he didn't need help at the moment, so I took my place at the end of a short line. Dunbar stood behind me.

The aroma of beef stew wafted on the air, and I was ready to eat.

Mullet stopped next to me, having served himself a bowl of stew with two biscuits on top. His sparse mustache was curved into a half-smile as he said, "Good grub. Better git some."

I thought it was apparent that I was standing in line for that very purpose, but I thought he was being friendly as a way of expressing sympathy for my getting the job of moving the rubbish. So I said, "Best idea I've had since breakfast."

He bobbed his head as he took in Dunbar and came back to me. " 'Bout enough news for a week in just two days."

"How's that?" I asked.

"The dame that run the beer parlor handed in her dinner pail."

Dunbar's voice was quick. "What do you mean?"

"Dead as a doornail. They found her just a little while ago."

"Who found her?" Dunbar's face was clouded like dark skies in the west.

"Don't know. Someone."

"What did it look like?"

"Don't know that, either. At first, they thought that fella Hodel mighta done it, but then someone said she was open for business yesterday. And of course, he was stone-cold dead the day before."

Dunbar's eyes had a hard cast. "We saw her in the middle of the day yesterday."

I recalled seeing him skip into The Bower with the three empty bottles and come right out. I said, "And we were gone the rest of the afternoon." As soon as I said it, I hoped no one pressed us for details about where we went. Now more than before, I didn't want to give away a witness.

"I'm going to see about this," said Dunbar. He left his place in line and headed for the center of town at a brisk pace.

Mullet stood watching with his mouth half-open.

Boots Larose appeared by his side. He was wearing his six-gun, which he often did when there was no need for it, and he had his thumb resting on the yellow handle. With his left hand, he stroked his chin beard. "He mighta been the last person that seen her alive."

"Oh, go on," I said. "I was with him."

"When he went in by himself?"

"You don't miss much," I said. "Does someone pay you to keep an eye out?"

"I didn't say who seen 'im. But you might say it's common knowledge." Larose gazed in the direction Dunbar had gone.

I said, "You know damn well—"

He crowded up next to me and swung his left elbow to hit me on the arm. "Don't tell me what I know, kid."

I settled back on my heels and took half a step backward.

An insolent expression crept onto his face. "I don't even know what kind of business she ran. For all I know, she sold more than beer and ale."

"That's a low thing to say about a woman who can't speak for herself anymore."

Larose gave a loose shrug. "Who's to say? All I know is that she's out of business now. But maybe it's a good opportunity for that lady with the French name."

I thought, *You wouldn't say that if Dunbar was here.*

Mullet blinked his eyes and said, "I'm gonna sit down and eat."

"Go ahead," said Larose. "I'll be there in a minute. I'm in line behind this kid."

Dunbar returned after the rest of us had gone back to work. He stopped at the wagon long enough to eat a bowl of stew standing up. When he joined me, he said, "It's true, all right. They

148

found Mary Weldon on the floor behind the bar where she served us. They think it happened sometime yesterday evening or last night."

"That's too bad," I said. "Does anyone have an idea how it happened?"

"Other than cast suspicion on me, which didn't last long, no."

"Boots Larose said something to that effect, that you were seen going in there by yourself. But anyone who knows that much also knows that I was right there and can testify that you weren't gone a minute."

"Oh, it's just talk. A distraction."

"Were there no signs, then?"

"No. In that respect, it's very similar to the way that George Hodel came to an end. Hand me the pitchfork, if you would."

I did as he asked. "Any idea of a reason?"

"The few people I talked to seemed mystified."

"And yourself?"

He stabbed at the pile and lifted out a mess of bottles and rags. "To me, it's apparent. But I need to keep myself from making assumptions or being convinced that my theory is the only one possible."

"And yours is—?"

"Again, similar to Hodel. I think Mary Weldon met her end because she seemed to know too much."

I used the shovel to scrape up a small heap of broken glass. "That she was the source of George Hodel's gossip, or that she heard things from him?"

"Could be either way. And let's not forget that she lent an ear to Bill Pearson as well."

I frowned. "But she said she didn't hear anything definite from him."

Dunbar jabbed the pitchfork into the pile again. "And I

believe her. But we'll mind how I phrased it. For seeming to know too much. Someone is worried about the truth coming out. That kind of fear makes people do desperate things."

I said, "It seems to me that someone might be going too far. Silencing people who may not know that much. For all we know, these last two people, at least, didn't know the whole truth. Even Verona doesn't know it for sure. She said so."

He dumped the rubbish into the wheelbarrow. "No, but that doesn't mean there isn't someone who does. And beyond that, the truth exists."

"You mean it's out there somewhere."

Dunbar nodded. "Yes. It's been there all this time, and nobody owns it."

I thought, *And somebody else might know.* In my mind, I had a picture of a terrified kid, the second sheepherder, running for his life to who knows where.

After we had worked more than two hours in the afternoon, Dunbar stuck the pitchfork in the pile and said, "I'll be back." With no further ceremony, he took off as before, except this time he headed for the Phelps Hotel. Some ten minutes later, he appeared, opening the door and moving aside out of view. Mrs. Deville stepped through the doorway into the sunlight, and Dunbar followed, carrying her Gladstone bag.

They crossed the street to the train station and waited. Some fifteen minutes later, a steam whistle announced the eastbound train. It slowed to a stop, let out a long hiss, and took on the single passenger. Dunbar waved his hat in farewell, and when the train chugged into motion, he waved it again. As the train receded and Dunbar walked toward me, I heard again the sawing and hammering of the work crew.

We labored on through the hot afternoon, using the pitchfork, the shovel, and our hands as necessary. We did not talk. I fell into my own thoughts, and I was sure Dunbar had fallen into his. I wondered if Mrs. Deville's departure had anything to do with recent events. I was sure it must, but I told myself not to make assumptions. I reminded myself that if two events happened in sequence, the first might or might not be a contributing cause of the second. And when there were three or more events, the relationship was even harder to determine.

I thought also about Mary Weldon and how unfair it was that her life was cut short. I remembered my earlier impression that she might have seen difficulties earlier in life and had found a garden of opportunity here in the dusty, windblown West. Now it seemed to me that the garden I had imagined, rather than having grapevines and fruit trees and a fountain, was a dark place with poisonous reptiles, lethal plants such as nightshade, and vines that shut out the daylight. The imaginary garden in back of The Bower had become a gloomy garden of sorrows.

In addition to not speaking, Dunbar did not sing or whistle all afternoon. Up until Mary Weldon's death, I had the impression that he already knew half of what people told him, and he always knew what to say or do in response. Now he did not convey that kind of self-assurance and control. I wondered if he felt, as I did, that we might have helped cause suspicion to fall on Mary Weldon. I also wondered if he had a plan.

At supper that evening, Dick Ainsworth paused to stand over Dunbar and me as we ate fried salt pork with white beans and cornbread. Ainsworth's chin was tucked toward his chest, and his knotted blue neckerchief had the effect of making his neck look shorter. I thought he was going to rebuke Dunbar for leaving during the work day, but he did not bear down on us as he so often did.

"I don't need both of you workin' on that trash pile tomorrow," he said. "The kid can finish it by himself." Motioning with his chin toward Dunbar, he continued. "You can go back to helping Bancroft."

I finished moving the rubbish heap the next morning at about eleven. No one paid me much attention as I put the tools away and walked toward the area where Dunbar and Del Bancroft had been working. When I drew close, I saw what I had gotten glimpses of throughout the morning. A crew of six men had been engaged in the building of a loading chute where the cattle would be run up out of the pens and into the railcars. At the moment, the construction had come to a standstill.

The crew consisted of Del and Dunbar, Larose and Mullet, and two men from a ranch near Hat Creek. Dick Ainsworth had joined the company, and now he and Del Bancroft were faced off and speaking in raised voices. As Mullet stood nearby, I moved close to him and asked what was going on.

He explained that Del and Ainsworth were arguing about how to put in the big or high end of the loading chute. It had two eighteen-foot posts that had to be sunk four feet into the ground. A heavy beam had to go across the top, and two three-inch planks had to go across the bottom of the chute. The walls of the chute had to have solid planking so that the steers would not see the train cars. It was the most massive structure in the project, and the big end next to the train cars had to be sturdy and accurate.

I moved closer to the spot where the big posts lay by the two holes, and I listened to the dispute. Del and Ainsworth were arguing back and forth about the procedure. Del wanted to sink the two posts, tamp them as plumb and even as possible, and put up the cross-members. Ainsworth wanted to assemble the two posts and the crossbeam on top and sink the two posts at the same time. Del said the assembly would be too awkward to handle and the plumbing and leveling would be too difficult as well. Ainsworth insisted that it would be too hard to put on the crossbeam later and that they would knock the posts out of plumb in the process.

The two men went around and around about one aspect and another, repeating themselves, with each one telling the other why he was wrong. I thought Del had a much better opinion, that it would be way too clumsy to manage two long, heavy posts with a heavy crosspiece on top, whether we were setting the posts into the holes or taking them out. He said that just about any post had to be lifted out of the hole at least once for the purpose of making the hole deeper or moving it an inch or so one way or another.

"Not if you do it right," said Ainsworth.

I remembered him telling me that I might have to reshape any hole in order to put the post in the right place. But I could see that he had set his mind to doing things in one way only, and he was going to make everyone else conform to his idea.

At length Del said, "I thought we had the agreement that on any part of the job I was doing, I would have the say-so about how we were going to do it."

"Maybe so," said Ainsworth. "But I've also been told that I've got the final word on any part of it. If something comes out wrong, I'm the one it comes back on."

Del had his chin set square. "We seem to be at loggerheads here."

"No need to be. If you don't like the way we're going to do things, you can go sulk in your tent."

"Don't be a fool," said Del. "You need every hand you can get if you insist on doing things your way. I'm glad we've got young Montgomery to help."

"If I need more, I'll call for 'em. But we're a sorry group if we can't do it with the men we've got right here."

Del shrugged. "Only so many men can get their hands on

one of these posts, anyway."

Ainsworth set men to measuring, boring with the brace and bit, and cutting the crosspieces. He sent me for the bolts and metal straps.

He not only made the men attach the top beam, but he also had them bolt on the two planks that would run under the chute, even though they could have been fitted just as well from the ground, once the posts were in place.

When we went to lift the structure the first time, it was more awkward and top-heavy than I expected. We slid the posts into the holes, and of course we had to lift the whole thing out in order to take out the dirt that fell in and to align the holes a little better. When we began to set the assembly into the holes again, Ainsworth ordered us to hold the lower ends up so we wouldn't push dirt in. That made the heavy end even more unwieldy, and it began to waver. We set the whole frame flat on the ground.

"This is where we'd like to have a capstan," said Larose.

Del folded his arms. "I don't know where you'd attach it, or how you'd get it or any other kind of block and tackle high enough."

Ainsworth said, "The same would go for getting that cross-beam up in the air."

Del shook his head. "It's only one piece. Not the whole damn thing."

"Let's try again," said Ainsworth. "Lift those ends up so they're clear of the sides of the hole, lift up the rest so it's straight up, and then lower the two legs down in."

We tried his method a couple of times, moving men from one position to another, but the top was too heavy and wobbly for us to set the whole thing straight up while keeping the lower ends free of the ground.

"Set it down," he said. "We'll use a rope."

He sent Mullet to the BC wagon. A few minutes later, Mullet returned with a one-inch hemp rope about fifty feet long. Larose tied it to the crossbeam and tossed the slack lengthwise between the posts and past the two holes. I did not see any good coming out of this plan, but I kept my thoughts to myself.

Ainsworth positioned the two Hat Creek men on one of the ends that went into a hole, and he put Del Bancroft and Mullet on the other end. He assigned Dunbar and me to the two corners that would go up in the air while he and Larose pulled on the rope. I thought, all this was going to do was put more pressure on the two pairs of men holding the lower ends of the posts.

And so it went. Ainsworth and Larose pulled while Dunbar and I pushed, and as soon as the crossbeam rose out of our reach, the structure began to weave. Dunbar and I stood by, ready to catch it if it began to come down.

Ainsworth and Larose pulled some more, and the top rose almost straight up. As I expected, the weight of all the lumber, plus the pressure exerted by the rope, caused the two pairs of men to stutter-step as the top began to totter. I was trying to watch everything at once, and I couldn't be sure, but it looked as if Ainsworth let the rope go.

Down came the structure with a *whoosh* and a *thud* and a *crack*. Dunbar and I jumped clear, and the other four men had the posts shaken from their grasp.

Dunbar put his hands on his hips and said, "What the hell happened?"

"It got away from us," said Ainsworth.

"If you'd been hangin' onto it, it would have pulled you forward."

Ainsworth's face hardened, and his neck seemed to shorten. "What do you mean? Do you think I did something on purpose?"

"It looked to me like you didn't try hard enough. I don't know why."

"Well, by God." Ainsworth had a glare in his eye as he stomped forward with his fists at his side. "Come over here and tell me you think I did something on purpose."

Dunbar walked close enough that either of them could have reached out and touched the other.

Ainsworth seethed. "Go ahead. Say it."

"I already did."

"You're saying I let the rope go on purpose."

"Don't put words in my mouth. I said I didn't think you tried hard enough to hold on, and I don't know why."

Ainsworth's flinty blue eyes roved over Dunbar, as if he was expecting him to make a move. "You know, I've got half a mind to send you back to Foster. We don't need troublemakers here."

Dunbar smiled. "Did Boots tell you what happened last week?"

"Don't worry about who told me what. But when someone works under me, I don't take back-talk."

Dunbar did not speak. He made a tiny motion with his gloved right hand, which hung at his side. It could have been one of those involuntary movements, like a twitch, or he could have been getting ready to ward off a fist.

"Don't even think of it," said Ainsworth.

Dunbar wasn't wearing a gun, so I imagined Ainsworth had heard that he packed a good punch.

Dunbar said, "You never know what someone is thinking. Even Boots Larose, who you think would stick up for you no matter what happened. Or these other four men. They watch you insist on doing something in a wrong-headed way, and some of them may wonder how the rope got away from you. You don't know what they think, and you can't tell them what or what not to think."

Ainsworth continued to glare. "I told you I can't have troublemakers around. I won't put up with you tryin' to set these other men against me. So I'm tellin' you and your little pal here to go pack your gear and go back to your ranch."

"Good enough," said Dunbar. "But it doesn't change anything that has happened."

Ainsworth's eyes narrowed. "Like what?"

"Just a general idea. You can apply it as you wish."

Dunbar and I sat around and drank another cup of coffee after the crew had gone back to work.

Dan said, "I don't know what problems he thinks he's solving. We're all going to be together for roundup before long, anyway. Some people don't think ahead very well. Maybe that's related to makin' others follow through with a bad idea." Dan shook his head. "I'm glad I wasn't there. Tryin' to hoist up something like that, with Boots Larose on the end of the rope. Did he let go, too?"

Dunbar raised his eyebrows. "Looked like it to me. And they were both wearing leather gloves. It's not as if they were trying to keep from getting rope burn."

"Fools at best," said Dan.

Dunbar gave a mild frown. "It's too bad it came to what it did. I would have liked to have seen this job through to the end. There's not that much left to do."

The three of us turned our attention to the corrals. The fresh lumber gleamed in the sun of late summer. I fancied again that the main gateway was superimposed on the catwalk, and I imagined Boots Larose pulling on the rope to bring them together.

CHAPTER ELEVEN

Dunbar and I returned to the shipping pens five days later to help Dan bring the chuck wagon back to the ranch. Most of the other workers had already left, and the site that had been bustling was now still and quiet, like a deserted village.

I climbed up onto the catwalk to appreciate the project. From above, the system of alleys, gates, and corrals looked like a maze. The planks were still bright and shiny, and the scent of new lumber hung in the air.

I took a complete 360-degree view of the layout. As I came back to the point where I started, something caught my attention two blocks away, in the shade in front of the mercantile. It was a moment like many I have had since then, in which I see something, realize that it is familiar, and take a second look to confirm what I had already registered without being conscious of it. Like seeing a cow in the mottled shade of low-lying box elder trees, or a deer in the shadow of a rocky bluff, I recognized the form and the essence of Emma.

I thought she recognized me as well. She raised her hand close to her face and made what I thought was a tentative wave. I raised my hand and waved, then hurried down the steps and across the bare ground where all the work activity had worn the grass away. I hoofed it to the other side of the street and turned left. I had no sense of the businesses I walked past until I came to The Missouri Primrose, where the sweet smell of whiskey drifted out through the open door. A few seconds later, I stopped in the shade of the overhang in front of the mercantile.

Emma was holding a book in front of her. She let go with her right hand as I moved my left hand toward her.

Her face was gleaming, and her eyes were shining. "So good to see you," she said.

"And for me, too. I didn't expect to find you here."

"We brought the wagon in. It's time to buy supplies, and my father can ride back with us."

"Nothing out of order on the way in?" I asked.

"No, but we kept our eyes open."

I didn't want to spoil our time together by telling her about the recent deaths, and I thought she would hear of them on her own if she hadn't already. I said, "How long will you be in town?"

"Not long. We'll go home this afternoon. And you?"

"The same. Dunbar and I came to help Dan with the wagon. We got word yesterday that the project was finished."

Her eyes carried an expression of mild surprise. "I thought you were here working on it."

"We were, but we got sent home early. Borden Crowley's foreman can be hard to get along with. Even your father had a disagreement with him."

"My father?"

"Yes, but he knew when to give in."

"Unlike Mr. Dunbar?"

"Why do you say that?"

She smiled, and her pretty teeth showed. "I wouldn't think you would do something to get the two of you sent home."

"You're right," I said. After a glance around, I continued. "I'll tell the story in more detail some other time. Oh. I just remembered something."

Her dark eyes quickened. "What is it?"

"I have something for you." I reached into my vest pocket

159

and drew out the little redstone figurine of a horse. "Mr. Dunbar found it and gave it to me. Said I might find something to do with it."

She held it in her palm. "How thoughtful of you. It's very pretty."

My nerve stood me in good stead. "For a pretty girl."

She lowered her eyes, and I saw her dark eyelashes.

"I didn't mean to be too forward," I said.

"I'm just shy." She raised her head and smiled.

"One of these days I'll—"

"You'll what?"

I felt as if I had put myself on thin ice. I needed to back up a little. "I'll try not to stand in front of a store window, where people can look out and see us."

I had let go of her hand earlier, and now I took it again. We moved aside a couple of yards so we were no longer in front of the window.

I said, "That's better. I don't feel that I'm being watched."

"What's to be seen?"

"Nothing." I glanced down at the book that she held. "Is that something you're reading?" I asked.

"Yes, it's by Jane Austen. It's called *Mansfield Park.*"

"Oh. I haven't heard of it. Didn't she write one called *Emma*?"

"Yes, she did. And *Pride and Prejudice* as well."

"Is this one about love and courtship, too?"

"So far, it's about a young girl who doesn't have much, and she has to go live with some well-to-do relatives. They have a country estate, and that's where the book takes its name."

"I see."

"She's made to feel like a servant at first. Rather sad, but we'll see how it goes." Emma paused. "You've read a little, haven't you?" Her dark eyes showed interest.

I could tell she wasn't just making conversation. I said, "A little. Not as much as you, I'm sure. The last couple of things I've read, in the past year, have been *The Oregon Trail* and *Two Years Before the Mast.* They're both interesting. They tell about the authors' experiences in their travels."

"We have Parkman at home," she said. "I've read *The Oregon Trail.* Some of it takes place not far from here."

"I'm sure the book you're reading now is interesting, too."

"Oh, yes. It's a novel, of course. Not real-life experiences. You've read novels, too, I'm sure."

I laughed. "Different kinds. When we were younger, we all read Harry Castlemon's books. That is, those of us who did any reading on our own. And I've read *Robinson Crusoe* and *Treasure Island.* Then there's *Uncle Tom's Cabin.* It's more serious than these others."

She nodded. "Oh, yes. It's important."

I hesitated as I glanced at the window. "I can't see if there's anyone looking out."

"You seem to be worried about that." She brushed away a wisp of hair.

"Well, I don't know if you'd want me to, anyway."

"Want what?"

My eyes met hers, and I tried to say something, but I couldn't. My lips moved, and I pressed her hand.

Her eyes softened and her eyelids closed as I moved toward her. A couple of seconds later, we drew apart, and we were two people standing in the sunlight looking into each other's eyes.

"That was nice," she said. She glanced over her shoulder toward the store window. "I don't mean to be in a hurry, but I think I should go."

"Me, too. I'm supposed to be working."

"Thank you for the little horse."

"I'm glad you like it."

"When will we see each other again?"

"I don't know. Probably when roundup's done."

"It'll be getting cold then. And we might be going to Lincoln."

I pressed her hand again. "We'll find time."

"Oh, yes." She let go of my hand and turned to walk into the store. Her single braid, sun-streaked, swayed as she moved. She slowed, made a partial turn, and said, "Good luck on roundup. Be careful."

I touched my hat brim. "The same to you. Good luck." I thought there was something purposeful in the way she told me to be careful, but I knew there were plenty of dangers in fall roundup—frost, snow, cold rain, and slippery ground for a horse to take a spill.

My gaze traveled past her as she disappeared into the store. Fifty feet away, leaning against the door jamb of The Missouri Primrose, Boots Larose slouched with a cigarette in his mouth. As I paused to observe him, he took a drag on the cigarette, flicked the butt into the street, stood up in a pose of tall boots and yellow-handled six-gun, and strode into the saloon.

Dunbar and I were greasing the wagon axles outside the barn when Bob Crenshaw and George Olney led their saddled horses into the open and made ready to mount up. They had stayed at the ranch all the time that Dunbar, Dan, and I had worked on the corral project, and Lou Foster was giving them a day off before we all went out on fall roundup.

George said, "We're gonna see how Bob's beezer holds up until I can get him into a cool, shady barroom."

Bob smiled and gave a dip of the head, then rubbed his red nose with his handkerchief. "There's dust and sagebrush everywhere I go, but as soon as we get some cold weather, I'll be better."

Dunbar stood with a smear of dark axle grease on his fingers.

"I'm never in a hurry for time to pass. Life goes by fast enough as it is. Old folks say the longer you live, the faster it goes. So for your sake, I'll hope that the cold weather comes early. For the sake of us workin' cattle, I wouldn't mind warm, clear weather through the season till we ship the steers."

"Thanks," said Bob. "Even cool weather helps."

"Enjoy yourselves in town," I said.

George paused as he turned out his stirrup. "I hope there's no trouble. At first, I was jealous of you two because you got to go to town and we didn't. But I sure don't like the sounds of what happened."

Dunbar rubbed his thumb against his two smudgy fingers. "It's no good. But I don't think a fellow would be in danger unless he let on that he knew something about what happened to Bill Pearson or the old horse trader years ago. Just a thought."

"Well, I don't know nothin' to begin with." George grabbed his saddle horn with both hands and pulled himself up and into the saddle.

Bob sniffled and said, "Neither do I. I don't talk about things I don't know anything about, and I don't ask questions."

I thought that was a good way to stay out of trouble. At the same time, I thought that keeping to oneself and not asking questions made it easier for someone else to get away with murder, as Mrs. Pearson had said. Rather than open up on that topic any more, I said, "If you happen to run into Boots Larose, you might want to tread light."

"What's with him?" asked George as he evened out his reins.

"He seems to be developing some kind of a grudge against Dunbar and me, and he might want to drag you into a conversation."

"Ha. Is he still sore about the boxing contest we had?"

"That and more," I said. "I'm not trying to tell you who to talk to or what to say. Just a word or two that he's got a chip on

163

his shoulder."

"We'll go light with him. Ready, Bob?"

"Sure thing." Bob mounted up and fell into place alongside George. Their horses picked up their feet, and the two cowhands took off for town.

Dunbar and I went back to work at getting the roundup wagon ready. We filled the water kegs and jugs, tied a stout tent pole onto each side of the wagon, and rolled out the canvas to check it for rips, tears, and mouse holes. The chuck box was clean from recent use and was ready to go. With everything in order, we moved to the bunkhouse, where we had a few hours of grinding coffee ahead of us.

Dunbar and I had finished washing the dishes and were sitting in the lamplight at the bunkhouse table. He was reading a newspaper, and I was reading a book.

"What's that you're engrossed in?" he asked.

"It's called *The Strange Case of Dr. Jekyll and Mr. Hyde.*"

"How do you come to be reading that?"

"Well, I thought I should be reading something, and I found it in a box of stuff tucked under one of the cots. It's in good condition. Not all the pages are cut. It looks like someone started it and didn't finish it."

"How do you like it?"

"It's something different for me."

"It's not James Fenimore Cooper, that's for sure."

"Or *Treasure Island,* either. It's hard to believe that the same author wrote both of them. But that was the reason I decided to read this one."

"It would be a surprise, all right. You get to expecting something similar when you pick up another book by the same author."

"Up until now." I reflected on some of our earlier conversations. "Is there an author you have as a favorite?"

"I can't say that I have one to the exclusion of another. I can take 'em dead serious, like Thomas Hardy, or I can take a mixture of sentimentality and peculiarity, like Charles Dickens."

I said, "I've read *Oliver Twist*, but I don't know Thomas Hardy."

"Gloomy stuff. Not Gothic, like *Jekyll and Hyde* or *Franken-stein*, but pessimistic. Tragedy in the provinces."

"Where everyone ends up miserable."

"That's right."

I was amused once again by how cheery he became when we talked about morbid topics. "Anything good in the newspaper?" I asked. "Any hangings?"

Dunbar winced. "Not in this edition, I'm glad to say. I'm not as fond of those things in real life, close to home."

Dan sat at the end of the table when he was done putting away the pots and pans. He said, "Enjoy the comfort, boys. You'll miss it when we're out on the range and the weather turns wet and cold."

I said, "That's not the only thing I'm dreading. I don't look forward to another three or four weeks in the company of Crowley's men."

"It's just part of the work," said Dan. "You can't expect to like everyone when you get a bunch of men like that together."

Dunbar smoothed out the newspaper on the table. "What about Crowley?"

"Oh, I don't think he'll be there very much. He leaves most of the work to his men."

"He does make himself scarce," said Dunbar. "He's not easy to get to know."

Dan raised his eyebrows. "It's hard to tell what's there. He keeps to himself. Never been married, as far as I know. He doesn't socialize. Doesn't drink."

"Oh."

"I think you could say he's pretty guarded. One of those fellows who's afraid that if he has a drink or two, he'll let something slip about what he's really like. Like some men who come from a low way of life, and don't want anyone to know it. My old man used to say, never trust a man who doesn't drink." Dan laughed. "Then he'd add, never trust a man who does, either."

A haze of smoke hung in the morning lamplight in the bunkhouse, and the air was heavy from the heat of the cookstove, the aroma of fried bacon and potatoes, and the fumes from the kerosene lantern. Bob was drinking his fourth cup of coffee, but it didn't seem to be doing him much good. His eyes were swollen and watery, and his face was flushed. He dabbed at his nose with his handkerchief every ten or fifteen seconds.

Lou took a puff on his cigarette. "You don't look so good, Bob. How much beer did you drink?"

"Not that much, but I think it might have made things worse. We rode through a lot of sagebrush, and just about every weed in the world is ripe right now."

Dunbar said, "The atmosphere in general is heavier at this time of year. As far as that goes, it might help the air in here if we opened a door."

"Go ahead," said Dan. "It's not that cold outside."

Dunbar rose from his seat, crossed the room, and opened the front door.

Lou said, "Bob, I think you'd better stay inside today. Help Dan with anything he needs. Bard can ride out with George."

The sunrise was casting a yellow glow against the light blue sky in the east when we rode out of the ranch. I was riding a speckled gray horse from my string, and I was keeping alert to see if he was going to try to step out from under me.

As soon as we were well out of earshot, George began plying me with questions about Dunbar—who he was, where he came from, what kind of a past he had, and whether he had a tendency to thump other men.

Because I didn't know much about Dunbar, I found it easy to give minimal answers. In response to the last question, I said, "You must have heard some talk about him in town."

"I heard he beat the tar out of Boots Larose for sayin' somethin' about a woman."

"I was there. He hit him only once. You know how stories are. The more they get told, the more they grow."

"Ain't that the truth?"

We split up on our ride, went out on a circular pattern, and met as planned. One thing we were supposed to be on the lookout for was any stock with Bill Pearson's brand. I didn't see any, and George said he didn't, either.

On my second circle, I rode past the Pearson homestead. It looked the same as it did the day Dunbar and I stopped by almost three weeks earlier, with the exception that it seemed even more forlorn. The door of the house was still tied shut with a piece of telegraph wire, and a low ridge of blow sand had gathered on the doorsill. Not a bird or rabbit was in sight, and only a few chicken feathers were caught in the weeds along the corral.

When I met up with George again, the sun was climbing high and heating up the day. I said, "We're not far from Blue Wolf Spring. It wouldn't hurt to water our horses."

George agreed, so we took the fifteen-minute detour. As we approached the spring, it had the same appearance as always. The low clay bluffs, narrow canyon, cropped chokecherry trees, and pocked damp earth all appeared as before. The scene gave me the feeling that the land remained constant, in spite of whatever malice men carried with them as they traveled over it.

I imagined Ainsworth and Larose out on the range somewhere, devising their next move against Dunbar and perhaps me.

We loosened our cinches and let the horses drink. While George rolled a cigarette and smoked it, I observed the area around us with its cow pies, bleached bones, and old foundation stones. I wondered if the ghost of Alex Garrison haunted the place. I thought that if it did, it did not bear any ill will to the likes of us.

We tightened our cinches and mounted up. The speckled gray horse was not giving me any trouble, and I thought the ride had done a good job of wearing him down a little. George's brown horse was sweating as well. The sun had climbed high enough that we decided to meander back to the ranch instead of trying to fit in another loop.

As we rode along, the heat of the sun reflected from the ground, and it seemed held down by the heavy air above. For miles around, not a tree was in sight—only small hills and bluffs here and there. We veered straight south to go around the back side of one low bluff, and out of habit I drew rein before I rode out into the open.

Off to the right a quarter of a mile, where the land sloped down to a trail that ran in a north-south direction, a buckboard rolled along, pulled by two dark horses. Two men sat on the seat, and I saw in an instant that the taller one, dressed in light-colored clothes and hat, was Borden Crowley.

A minute later, I identified the man handling the reins as Fred Mullet. I imagined he was driving the boss to town to stock up on provisions for roundup, and as before, I pictured Larose and Ainsworth off on their own, hatching a plan.

For the moment, I thought it was just as well not to show ourselves. I believed we were still on Crowley's land, and although no one would begrudge us for watering our horses at a spring on his property, I did not know how touchy he would be.

So I signaled to George to hang back and be quiet. We dismounted and held our reins. I put my hand over the nose of the speckled gray horse.

As the wagon moved closer, voices rose on the air. Crowley's voice had a tone of anger, and Mullet's answers were short and muffled. George and I looked at each other and waited.

A minute later, Crowley's voice became more audible. "You're just a stupid son of a bitch! You never know when to keep your mouth shut. Why don't you learn somethin'? You gonna be a jackass all your life?"

I could not pick out the mumbled response.

Crowley's voice cut the air. "Don't make me mad, you idiot! You've got to be the dumbest ass in the world. Whose business is it, anyway?"

The sounds of the horses and the wagon wheels subsided enough for me to hear Mullet say, "I didn't think it would do any harm."

"You didn't think! That's your problem! You don't think! You make me so damn mad I could choke you!" Crowley held a kind of walking stick upright between his knees, and he pounded it on the floor of the buckboard. "Stop this wagon!" he hollered.

The wagon halted, out in the middle of an empty rangeland.

"Now get out!"

"What for?"

"Get down!"

I could see Mullet's frowning face as he said, "Why?"

Crowley's voice rose even louder. "Because I said so!"

Mullet handed him the reins and climbed down. "Now what am I supposed to do?"

"I don't care! You can stand there for the rest of your life, or you can walk back to the ranch."

Mullet stood without speaking.

Crowley shook the reins, and the wagon moved forward. It

did not go ten yards before it stopped. Crowley turned in the seat, using the stick to steady himself.

"Don't be a fool! Are you going to stand there like an idiot?"

"I don't know what you want me to do."

"Get up here and drive this wagon. Just keep your mouth shut the rest of the way to town, and don't make me mad."

"Yes, sir."

George and I exchanged another glance. The wagon creaked as Mullet climbed aboard, and a few seconds later it rolled away.

George told the story about Crowley and Mullet that same day at noon dinner. Gossip being a main stock in trade with him, he wouldn't have been able to keep it in much longer. When he finished the story, he said, "I've seen men fly into a fit like that and not make any sense. My old man was like that, but he was drunk when he did it. This was in the middle of the day, and from what I've heard, Crowley doesn't drink."

Lou Foster said, "He doesn't."

Dan whacked the wooden spoon on the lip of the pot of beans. "It's the vapors. They get to some people. Rise up from down in the guts and work their way up to the brain."

George shook his head. "Well, I'm glad I don't work for him."

The sun was making its fast drop at the end of the afternoon, casting an orange glow in the western sky. Dunbar and I were sitting outside the bunkhouse and waiting for the supper bell to ring. Dan had made biscuits, and even though he had the front and the back door open, the air inside was stifling. I was making my way through a few pages of *Dr. Jekyll and Mr. Hyde,* and Dunbar was reading another old newspaper he had found. Not far from where we sat, Bob and George were playing a game of checkers on a board they balanced on their laps.

The sound of horse hooves on dry ground caused all four of us to look up. Boots Larose rode into the ranch yard by himself, sitting straight up on a bright sorrel horse with a white blaze and four white socks. Larose himself wore his tall, dark brown boots with mule-ear tabs, and I wouldn't have been surprised to learn that he had stopped a quarter-mile back to shine them.

He rode past the bunkhouse without looking our way, much less waving. He rode up to the ranch house, dismounted, tied his horse, and knocked on the door.

Lou Foster appeared at the doorway, and after a brief exchange, he took the small envelope that Larose handed him. I assumed it had to do with the upcoming roundup, as they both acted as if the exchange was routine and expected.

With no further ceremony, Larose returned to his horse, taking long and definite strides that made his spurs jingle. He pulled the reins loose from the hitching rail, flicked them into place, and sprang up into the saddle. I thought he would rein the horse around, but he gigged it straight ahead and rode out of the ranch yard at the far end, past the cookshack end of the bunkhouse. I imagined he went that way so he wouldn't have to ride past the four of us again.

The maneuver was not lost on George and Bob. They both looked up and stared.

George twisted his mouth and said, "Boots must be in a hurry."

I thought I detected a dry tone as I recalled our conversation from earlier in the day.

"It's all right," said Dunbar. "We'll have plenty of time for fellowship in the next few weeks."

"Just as well. He won't be comin' to us and wantin' to stay in our tent when the rain starts drizzlin'. Or yours, either. I guess I shouldn't say that, but it seems to me that Boots isn't as friendly as he used to be."

Bob sniffed and ran the sleeve of his shirt across his nose. "It's the company he keeps."

A picture of Dick Ainsworth rose in my mind, with his tight presence and hard stare. Cold, wet weather and slippery ground would be bad enough in the coming weeks, and the prospect of fellowship, as Dunbar put it, made for another kind of dark cloud.

CHAPTER TWELVE

At our first roundup camp, I helped set up the tent off the end of the chuck wagon. The afternoon was warm without much of a breeze, but Dan wanted to show the new night wrangler the routine of setting up the canopy, so I helped.

I was glad not to have the job of night wrangler this time. It was the lowest job on the roundup crew. Not only did the nighthawk have to watch the horse herd, but in the daytime, he had to help the cook move camp and set up. He also had to fetch water and firewood. For sleep, he grabbed what bits of time he could find. The job was ragged enough during spring roundup, but in the fall, the nights were longer and colder, which meant that the snatches of rest were shorter and colder.

My good luck came in part from Del Bancroft being the roundup boss this fall. Each outfit contributed workers in proportion to its size and holdings, and a couple of new hands were hired on. This season, the night wrangler was new, as was the day wrangler. The riders went out in pairs to ride circles in the gather, so I was paired with Dunbar.

After meeting up with the other outfits and setting camp the first day, we set out at sunrise on the second day. Dunbar had brought both of his horses, so he was riding his blue roan. He had the horse's neck rope coiled and tied to the left side of his saddle, while he had his stock rope or catch rope tied to the right. He wore riding gloves and had his pistol on his hip.

I rode the bay horse from my string. I wanted a horse that

wouldn't give me trouble on the first day, and he was a good choice. He was calm and gentle, but he could run when I wanted him to, and he had good endurance. Though the days were still warm, they were growing shorter, and a briskness carried on the morning air. It made some horses frisky. It also put me in mind to tie a canvas jacket onto the back of my saddle and to wear a wool shirt. I had my gloves tucked under my belt, and my pistol and holster lay tucked away in my saddlebag. I did not have the habit of toting a gun, and I had not developed a comfortable way for it to ride on my hip while I was in the saddle.

As we rode out, I rehearsed the work ahead. As a general rule, during fall roundup, we did not gather cows with branded calves. This was beef roundup, so we gathered steers to be shipped to Omaha. While we were at it, we brought in stock that needed to be branded or re-branded. Every day or so we would brand, and we would let go any stock that we did not intend to drive to the shipping pens.

Dunbar and I split up a couple of miles from camp, each to ride on his own circle. As I turned north, I caught a view of the morning sun. It had cleared the hills in the east, and the pink sky of sunrise had given way to yellow and blue.

I passed up a couple of cow-calf pairs and rode on to find my first animal to herd, a rangy steer with lean hips and foot-long horns. I spurred my horse, slapped my leg, and shouted, "Hee-yaw!" as I headed him toward camp. The bay horse knew what to do, and with his help, I launched into the fall season's work of being a cowpuncher.

Two hands from the Bonner ranch were holding the herd on the bedding ground as I drove five head of cattle in from my ride. Three were steers, and the other two were a branded cow with an unbranded calf. I turned them all into the herd and headed to the cavvy ground, where I could unsaddle my horse. I saw Dunbar's blue roan in the cavvy, standing head-to-head with the buckskin. I stripped my horse, left my rigging where it would not be in the way, and walked to camp. My legs felt light and bowed as they do after a time in the saddle, and my stomach reminded me that I hadn't eaten for more than six hours.

The roundup crew consisted of eighteen riders, the two wranglers, and Dan, the cook. The BC outfit had five riders present—Ainsworth, Larose, Mullet, and two others. They sat on the ground in a group by themselves and paid no attention to me or Dunbar. I thought that was a good beginning.

When I brought in my second gather in late afternoon of the same day, Del Bancroft met me on horseback. He was wearing a hat, gloves, and chaps, as well as a shirt with a full row of buttons and two chest pockets. I thought he looked quite like a roundup boss. His teeth showed as he smiled and then spoke.

"Afternoon, Tag. Don't put your horse away yet. We've got enough to brand already, so you stand by."

As a crew, we did not yet have a routine set, but the usual practice would be to have one or two men cut the animals from the herd, one or two rope, and one or two brand. Del took stock of who was on hand, and he assigned our tasks. Dunbar and I sat by on our horses to go after anything that got loose. Mullet and Larose were going to cut and rope, the two men from Hat Creek would wrestle and hold the stock, and Ainsworth and Del were going to brand.

The first couple of animals went through all right. Bawling and braying filled the air, along with the pungent smell of burned hair. Larose cut out the third animal, a steer that weighed about seven or eight hundred pounds and needed to be re-branded. As soon as the steer emerged from the herd, it cut to the right and began running.

175

Mullet took off in pursuit, shaking out a loop. He didn't throw right away, and the loop grew. When he made his throw, the steer lowered its head and picked up its feet at just the right moment, and it ran through the loop. By the time Mullet pulled his slack, he caught only the right hind leg. The steer bolted, yanking the rope from Mullet's grasp, and headed for the open plain with the rope trailing.

Dunbar, riding the buckskin, sprang into action. He took down his rope from the right side, shook out a loop, and roped the steer by the horns. He gained on the steer, shook his slack over the steer's back and onto its right hip, turned his horse to the left, and tripped the steer. The buckskin continued dragging, to keep the steer from getting up. Dunbar dismounted, ran back to the steer, and untied Mullet's rope. The buckskin kept tension on the rope until Dunbar re-mounted and faced the horse toward the steer. When he moved the horse forward, the steer scrambled to its feet. Dunbar rode ahead, tightening the rope again, and led the steer toward the branding fire. The steer danced along, straining back, but it followed.

Meanwhile, Mullet had recovered his rope and made ready to catch the steer by its hind feet. He caught it on his second toss. He and Dunbar stretched the animal out, and Del branded it.

Larose and I rode up on either side, ready to haze the steer into the herd.

"That was slick," said Mullet. "Did you see the way he tripped that steer?"

Larose took a long sniff. "Oh, yeah. Just about any hand that come up the trail can do that. I learned from an old vah-kerro. But it's not just any old hand that can trip 'em from the front."

Mullet's mouth hung open as it sometimes did. "Really? I'd like to see that. Kin you do it?"

Larose shrugged, as if modesty was his nature. "Haven't done it in a while."

"Why don't you show us?"

Larose motioned with his head toward the steer. "I don't think this fella has got much play left in him at the moment."

"We'll cut out another one."

"Nah. Leave it be." Larose waved his hand.

"I'd like to see it." Mullet smiled as he glanced around. By now, a few other men had gathered to watch, so he said, "We all would. Don't you think?"

A couple of the other men said, "Sure," and "Why not?"

"Leave it be," said Larose. "We have enough real work to do."

Mullet was wearing his simpleton's smile. "How about you, Dunbar? Do you know how to trip 'em from the front?"

"I didn't learn from an old *vaquero*, but I do know how."

"Ha, ha," said Mullet. "Let's see it."

By now, George Olney had joined the group of onlookers. "Oh, yes," he said. "We can even take wagers. Who'd like to bet that he can, and who'd like to bet that he can't?"

Dunbar held up his hand. "Let's not do it for money. Just for sport. Anyone else who wants to can give it a try as well."

Now Mullet was happy. He asked for someone to point out a steer that was a real buster, and when the re-branded steer was back in the herd, Mullet cut out the one that was recommended.

As the fresh steer came to the edge of the herd, I saw that it was at least as large as the previous one. It was brownish black and husky, and it moved its head from one side to another as it looked for an opening. As the steer broke free, Mullet slapped it with the loop end of his rope and hollered, "Yahhh!"

The steer bolted, and Dunbar followed on the buckskin. As before, he rode up on the left side and made his throw. He settled the loop on the steer's horns, then sped up as he shook out slack beyond and in front of the steer's head. As he slowed and sagged back, the rope fell in front of the steer and tripped it. The animal flew in the air, head over heels, and landed with a thud and a grunt that I could hear from fifty yards away. As the steer came to its feet, Dunbar rode forward and shook slack into his rope. He shook again, and the rope came free.

The steer was already branded, so Mullet and I hazed it back to the herd and pushed it in.

By now, Dick Ainsworth had walked onto the scene. He stood in front of Mullet's horse and said, "Are you through fooling around? There's work to do, you know."

"Aw, hell," said Mullet. "It wasn't but a minute or two, and it's not every day you get to see something like that."

"Don't talk back to me. I might not be the boss on this roundup, but I'm still your foreman. Don't forget where you come from, because that's where we go back to when this thing is over and we've got the steers shipped." Ainsworth made his dry spitting sound. "At least Boots knows better than to fool around."

Dunbar had coiled his rope and was riding toward me at a walk. The buckskin's breathing was audible, but the horse looked loose and relaxed.

Ainsworth shifted so that he had his back turned to Dunbar.

Dunbar spoke to me. "Let's go back and take our posts, and the others can get under way again with the day's branding."

Mullet spoke past Ainsworth and toward us. "Dunbar, that was pretty damn good. Just goes to show, you don't know what a man's got in him, just to look at him." He raised his head as he smiled at me.

"Ain't that right, kid?"

I was searching for an answer, but Ainsworth saved me the trouble.

He said, "You talk too much, Mullet."

★ ★ ★ ★ ★

A week into the roundup, halfway through the second half of September, a slow, cold, wet spell of weather came in. Cold rain turned to sleet and went back to rain. The short grass was slick, and the muddy ground was slicker. Work came to a standstill until the weather cleared up. The men who did not have to be out on shift watching the herds were gathered under the canvas tent. Nearby, the cookfire threw out thick clouds of smoke, so the air beneath the canopy was heavy with the mixed odors of woodsmoke, wet wool clothing, wet leather, and old sweat.

A couple of men sat on crates, a few including myself sat on folded saddle blankets, and the rest stood around. No one spoke much, and if a newcomer had stepped under the canvas awning, he would have sensed right away that humor was in short supply.

At the rear of the tent, standing at the tailgate mixing dough, Dan turned and said, "This is a hell of a time to mention it, but we're going to run out of beef."

Del Bancroft tipped back his hat. "It's not so bad in one sense. At least we have time to butcher one."

Ainsworth cleared his throat. "Sure. We can divvy up the work. Boots, you and Mullet can cut out that heifer, and a couple of others can do the butcherin'." His dark blue eyes bore down on me. "This lad here, and maybe someone else. Just a suggestion."

A dozen pair of eyes fell on me. "I can do my share," I said.

Ainsworth turned to Larose. "You know the heifer that we held back for that purpose, don't you?"

"Sure. Brockle face, walks with a gimp."

"That's the one. You and Mullet can cut it out of the herd, lead it over to where you're going to kill it, and drop it there."

I stood up and stepped around Ainsworth. I said to Dan, "If you give me the knives, I'll go do this work."

"Thanks, kid. I appreciate it." He took out the knives that he kept for that purpose, and he handed them to me.

With the knives in hand, I went out into the cold drizzle and selected a place away from the camp and away from the herd. There I waited for Mullet and Larose to show up. I realized I could have stayed in the tent until they saddled their horses, but that time had passed, and I figured they would make as short a work of it as possible. So I stood like a fool with my hands drawn up inside the sleeves of my jacket, with slow, cold rain falling around me.

After a while they came looming out of the mist with a chubby heifer limping along at the end of a rope. When they reached the spot where I stood, Larose swung down from his horse and swaggered forward. He tossed a cigarette butt aside onto the wet grass. I had not liked his careless way of smoking on the range, and even though I knew it wouldn't start a fire at the moment, I didn't care for his present gesture.

Mullet sat hunched in the saddle, holding the rope, while Larose's horse stood with the reins on the ground.

"Here's how you do it," said Larose. He drew his yellow-handled pistol, raised it, and cocked it. "You wait until they look straight at you, and then you give it to 'em."

After a long moment, the heifer lifted its head, lolled, and gazed forward. The gun blasted, and the animal cleared the ground by three inches with all four feet and fell onto its side.

"That's with cattle," said Larose. "With horses it's a little different." His own horse had lurched away, run a few yards, and stopped. He holstered his gun and walked away toward his mount.

I went to work on the animal. I had butchered on the ground before, so I knew how to go about it, turning the animal from one side to another as I skinned it. I was getting started on the first front hock when I heard a swishing sound behind me. I dropped the foot, straightened up, and turned around.

Dunbar was wearing a canvas capote with the hood up over his head. Moisture was gathering on his dark mustache. "Thought you could use a hand."

"Thanks. I can. Sorry to see you out in the wet and cold, though."

"Not so bad. Just part of divvying up the work."

Aside from getting wet and developing a sore back, I didn't mind the work. It kept me away from the close company of Ainsworth and Larose for a couple of hours, and the smell of fresh warm meat in the cold air was not disagreeable. As for humor, it still seemed distant. Dunbar did not speak much, and he did not indulge in his whimsical and morbid comments as he had done in the past. But as I was finishing up, and he dragged away the feet, head, and guts, I thought I heard him humming the tune about the woman who died in the snow.

The weather cleared out, and the days warmed up, but the nights stayed cold. Freezing temperatures, along with the humidity from the recent rain, made for slow drying of wool garments, cold leather on saddles and straps, and cold, stiff ropes. Dunbar and I took our ropes into our tent at night and kept them under our blankets. In the morning we warmed our horses' bits by holding the bridles inside our coats. Even at that, sometimes a webbed cinch had frozen before it dried out, and the horse would rear up in the morning when I pulled the latigo.

Men who did not have tents but slept under tarpaulins had it even more difficult. They awoke with frost on the canvas that covered them. They held their ropes close to the fire in the morning, trying to make them more pliant. They said that their beds never dried out, even on sunny days when they spread the blankets on sagebrush.

As we moved into October, the days became shorter a few

minutes at a time. Shadows became darker; dusk, thicker. The cold wind blew out of the northwest, and we didn't know when the next storm would come.

Each sunny day seemed like a short reprieve. Meanwhile, the herd of animals to be shipped grew by the day, and Del Bancroft reminded us that we would have a short end to the season, for instead of having to drive the cattle all the way to Chadron, as in years past, we had only to drive them to the shipping pens in Brome.

Borden Crowley rode into the roundup camp at noon on a warm October day. The crew had made a swing west and north, and now that the operation was moving south and east, it was close enough for Crowley to ride out from his ranch. As soon as he appeared, Mullet jumped and made haste to the bed wagon, where he took out a small canvas bag that held the three-legged camp stool with the leather seat. At that moment I realized that the BC crew carried the stool on the whole campaign in order to accommodate their boss at such moments as he might choose to drop in.

Crowley dismounted a few yards out and handed his reins to the day wrangler. He stood for a minute and surveyed the camp with a peculiar air I had noted about him, as if he wanted to be admired at the same time that he avoided men who were not of his immediate circle. Taller than average and neither lean nor heavy, decked out in a hat the color of dull silver and a jacket and vest to match, and a pair of light-gray wool pants, he looked as if he could have been a land speculator or an investor on a ditch project.

Mullet set the camp stool in place, and Crowley walked forward to take a seat. He glanced around and nodded at the hands who were seated and eating their grub, but his brown eyes did not rest on anyone. They glided over Dunbar and me, then raised to meet Dan, who handed him a tin plate heaped with a chunk of fried beef and a side of fried potatoes.

"Thanks," he said. He stared at the grub for a long moment until he leaned to one side and took out a pocketknife. After another fifteen seconds, he opened the knife and cut into the chunk of beef. In a way, he was a neat man, reserved in his motions and always clean-shaven, but his hair, a mix of mousy brown and gray, had a dull, matted texture suggesting that he did not wash it often, and his fingernails were not trimmed or clean. I found myself wincing, then looked away at the campfire coals, lest he see me watching.

I put Borden Crowley and his men out of my mind as I finished my meal. After a cup of coffee, I was ready to pick out a horse for the afternoon ride.

As Dunbar and I reached the horse herd, the day wrangler met us with a troubled expression on his face. Directing his words toward Dunbar, he said, "I don't mean to be startin' anything, but I think you should know that Boots Larose tried to rope out your blue roan like he wanted to ride it. I told him not to."

"When was this?"

"A few minutes ago. He went back to the camp. Maybe he wanted to ask Dick Ainsworth somethin'."

Dunbar turned square around and headed for the wagon. I thought there might be trouble, for he did not have his calm demeanor, so I walked alongside him.

"We want to be careful," I said. "They might be trying to bait you."

His dark mustache was firm, and his eyes were hard as flint. "I know."

Half a dozen men were still sitting on the grass or leaning on one elbow as we marched into camp. Boots Larose had his back to us as he stood talking to Dick Ainsworth, both of them less than a foot away from Borden Crowley's elbow as he carved at the meat on his plate. Mullet stood on the other side of Crowley, as if he was waiting for orders.

Dunbar stopped, and his voice had a challenging tone as he called out, "Larose, I've got somethin' to say to you."

Larose looked over his shoulder and raised an eyebrow.

"Don't give me your back. Turn around and look at me like a man."

Larose drew back with his left foot, made a slow rotation, and came into position with his right hand near the yellow handle of his six-gun. With his left hand, he tossed the snipe of a cigarette onto the grass near his foot. "What do you need?"

"The wrangler told me you tried to put a rope on my horse."

Larose stretched his face downward in his insolent way. "Which horse was that?"

"You know damn well which one. The blue roan."

"Ah. That one. I didn't know whose it was."

"You know whose it is, and you know damn well not to touch another man's horse without his permission."

Larose raised his chin. "I thought it was an extra horse in the cavvy, didn't belong to anyone's string in particular."

"That's a preposterous thing to say."

Larose shrugged. "Call it what you want."

Dunbar took a breath. I could see he was trying to keep himself calm, but he was not going to let the offense go. He said, "I'll call it a lie."

Time stood still. Mullet stood gaping with his mouth open. Crowley stared straight ahead, his hand poised with his knife stuck into the remaining piece of meat. Ainsworth's dark blue eyes were fixed on Dunbar, but he had not stepped into the clear. He and Larose and Crowley were bunched up. Larose's face had fallen at Dunbar's words, and now he had to say or do something.

He took in a breath, tipped his head, and said, "What are you goin' to do about it?"

"I don't have to do anything," said Dunbar. "But if you want to step up and take a swipe at me, give it a try." Dunbar motioned with his head. "Or, if you want to go for your gun, you can try that. One thing I know. When a man knows he's in the right, he's got a better chance of comin' out on top." Dunbar's dark eyes moved to Crowley and Ainsworth, then back to Larose. "And when a man knows the truth is against him, he doesn't have enough in him."

Ainsworth spoke up. "You talk too much."

Dunbar waved his left hand. "Save that for your own men. You can't control what the rest of the world says, even though you'd like to."

No one spoke further. Mullet had closed his mouth and seemed still to be waiting for orders. Larose stepped on his cigarette butt, and Crowley returned to cutting his meat. Ainsworth was practicing his hard stare, but it did not have any effect as Dunbar and I headed back to the herd to pick out our horses for the afternoon's work.

CHAPTER THIRTEEN

With the main gate of the shipping pens wide open, we ran half of the horse herd, some fifty head, in first. The beef herd followed. Fall roundup was ending in a swift manner, as Del Bancroft had predicted. It was not hard to move a band of horses as long as a man on horseback stayed out in front, and a herd of shipping steers moved faster than a mixed herd of cows, calves, steers, and heifers.

Delivering the beef herd to the new shipping pens was a big event for the small town of Brome. Merchants and townsfolk lined the main street as if they were waiting for a Fourth of July parade. Others had come into town for the event. Lou Foster, clean-shaven and in clean clothes, leaned on his crutch and raised his head to watch the animals go by. Dunbar and I waved to him as we took up the rear of the herd of steers. When the big gate closed behind the last steer, Lou came hobbling up to us. We dismounted and shook hands with him.

Dunbar said, "They're sortin' the cattle into pens accordin' to the brands."

"Sure," said Lou. "I'm anxious to know how many head I've got, but I realize it'll take a little while to secure a count." In a lowered voice he asked, "Everything go all right? Any trouble?"

"Nothing to speak of," said Dunbar. "A couple of Crowley's men like to be difficult, but nothing came of it."

I thought Dunbar's comment was something of an understatement. I had spent many long moments in the past two

186

weeks wondering if Larose and Ainsworth had intended to set him up but couldn't quite follow through when the moment came. When nothing else happened from one day to the next, I wondered if they were waiting for a second opportunity.

"That's good." Lou shifted on his crutch. "I'm going to watch the men sort the cattle. I want to see what kind of shape the steers are in."

"Pretty good, overall." Dunbar moved his head to one side and another, as if he was keeping a lookout as he made easy conversation.

As Lou moved away, Dunbar turned to me. "I'll hold your horse if you'd like." He motioned with his head toward the hotel.

I followed the gesture, and my pulse jumped. Emma was standing next to her mother in front of the hotel. I handed Dunbar my reins and hurried over.

I was not surprised to see her, for a few men on the crew had written letters when we had a definite date for arriving with the herd. Del Bancroft had put a letter into the white canvas bag, and Dunbar had put in something as well, though I couldn't tell if it was one letter or two, he did it so discreetly.

When I reached the other side of the street, I took off my hat to say good afternoon to Emma and her mother. Mrs. Bancroft nodded but kept her eyes on the shipping pens where the bustling and thumping and men's voices rose on the air. I made a sweeping motion with my hat and gave a half-bow to Emma, and she laughed.

"I'm glad to see you made it back safe," she said.

"And I'm glad to see you." I reached forward and touched her hand as she held it toward me, but the presence of her mother caused me to withdraw my hand after a couple of seconds. "I can't stay long," I said. "I have to get back to work."

"Of course," she said. "I'll see you later."

I winked. "I'll keep an eye out for you."

As I turned to walk back to the corrals, I almost ran into a thin, nondescript fellow.

"Excuse me," I said.

"It's all right. I was told that you might be able to help me find Mr. Dunbar." His voice had a quaver to it.

I took a second to observe him with more attention. He was not very tall and wore a low hat, so I had to peer. He had stringy, dirty blond hair and furtive blue eyes. I would have guessed him to be about thirty years old. I thought he had a hollow expression on his face and a nervous demeanor in general, as his hands did not keep still.

"I can take you to him," I said. "Where did you come from?"

Still in his shaky voice, he said, "I came in on the westbound train. Got here at about noon."

"Today?"

"Yeh. I came with Mrs. Deville."

I stopped before I even started walking. I looked at this slip of a man with bony shoulders and stringy hair, and I had an urge to ask him how in the world he came about traveling with Mrs. Deville. But I held my tongue and thought better.

"Is she in the hotel?" I asked.

"Yes. She's in one room, and I'm in another."

I would have expected him to be sleeping in the stable, but I treated his statement as if it were as normal as sunshine. I said, "That's good. Let's go find Mr. Dunbar. He's over by the corrals." I led the way, and the newcomer followed at about half a pace behind me.

Dunbar was standing on the other side of the two horses he was holding. As he came into view, I said, "That's him, in the dark hat."

"Oh, yeah," said the man.

"Do you know him?"

"We met before."

I slowed down and let the stranger walk past me. If he knew Dunbar, he didn't need an introduction. And if he came to talk to Dunbar, he didn't need me listening in.

They spoke for a couple of minutes, each of them nodding by turns. Their voices rose in a tone of conclusion, and the small man walked away in the direction of the hotel.

I joined Dunbar and took the reins to the horse I had been riding, a shiny sorrel. I said, "I hope he's not looking for work. Half of us are going to be out of a job by this time tomorrow, and I don't know if there would be anything for him."

"He's all right," said Dunbar.

I did not dare say anything about Mrs. Deville, but I was hoping to catch sight of her.

"Shall we put our horses away?" I asked.

"I suppose. We ought to help these other fellows sort the cattle." Dunbar scratched his ear. "I'll tell you what. Why don't you put the horses away, and I'll be back in time to go help sort." He handed me the reins to the brown horse he had been riding.

"I can do that," I said. I thought some kind of fat was in the fire, and I needed to be on the lookout so I didn't foul things up.

With some men on the ground working gates and other men on horseback moving the cattle, we finished the sorting in late afternoon. Dust hung in the air, as did the smell of manure. Steers bellowed, and hooves thumped against corral planks. Del Bancroft and Borden Crowley stood on the catwalk, looking over the distribution of cattle in the pens. Lou Foster stood by the main gate, leaning on his crutch. Three other owners of small outfits were out in the pens. Dunbar and I stood near Lou, waiting for the crew to gather. This would be a time to say goodbye to men we had worked with, for some of them would be paid off today.

Crowley came down from the catwalk and joined up with his foreman, Dick Ainsworth. The two of them stood a few yards away from Lou Foster. Del Bancroft took another stroll down the catwalk and back, then came down the steps and joined the group.

Hired hands began to gather, and the other three owners stepped out through the gate. The group of six owners made a small arc facing the crowd of hired men. People from town approached and stood nearby in groups of twos and threes, some of them exchanging words with some of the cowhands. Other townspeople, like Otto Trent and Carl Granger, seemed to have come to be part of a public event. I had the sense that the crowd expected someone to make a speech, but no one made a move.

Del Bancroft looked to either side, and receiving nothing but shrugs and small shakes of the head from the other owners, he stepped forward. "I thought maybe someone was going to say something, but to tell you the truth, we hadn't planned anything. But for my part, I can say I'm very pleased to see this set of corrals here and the cattle in the pens." He paused. "I guess that's about all I have to say. Does anyone else—"

Dunbar stepped away from the crowd and spoke in a clear voice. "While we're all here, I wouldn't mind making a small presentation. Won't take but a couple of minutes." He waved in the direction of the hotel.

The crowd turned to see Mrs. Deville beginning to cross the street with a heavier, slow-moving person at her side. I recognized Verona and her walking stick.

Borden Crowley spoke out. "Oh, come on, now. We don't have time to waste. The day's slipping away."

Dunbar dismissed him with a wave. "This won't take long."

Verona and Mrs. Deville made quite a pair as they approached us—Verona in her work clothes, leaning on a stick that had been cut from the wild, and Mrs. Deville, in a black jacket, a white blouse, and a long black wool skirt.

"Thanks for coming," said Dunbar when they came to a stop.

Mrs. Deville smiled and moved back a step.

Verona moved her lips in a way that toothless people do, though I knew she had teeth. She did not speak.

Del Bancroft said, "If you don't mind, we do need to move along. Could you state your business? Some of these men are waiting to be paid, and some of them are waiting to be let go for the day."

In a voice that she seemed to be trying to keep steady, Verona said, "Mr. Dunbar invited me."

Borden Crowley's eyes narrowed as they moved from Verona to Dunbar. I thought I saw a strange flicker of recognition, and then his face went expressionless, as I had seen it before.

Dunbar gave Verona a faint smile and said, "A little while back, you told me a story about something that happened many years ago. I'd like you to tell that story again now."

A murmur went through the crowd. I looked around to keep track of Boots Larose, and I saw him standing behind Dick Ainsworth and Borden Crowley.

Ainsworth spoke out. "For God's sake, let's get back to business."

Dunbar nodded to Verona. "Go ahead."

Verona cleared her throat, coughed, and spoke. "It was about fifteen years ago. One day I was out at Alex Garrison's place, along about evening, and a kid came by on foot. He was scared to death. He said he had been working in a sheepherders' camp up on Old Woman Creek, and a stranger rode into their camp. At night. The stranger said he had come to kill sheep, but he didn't seem to have the nerve, and the sheepherder made fun of him. So the stranger flew into a fit, came down from his horse, and clubbed the sheepherder to death."

Verona paused with her tongue stuck to the bottom of her upper lip.

Dunbar said, "And then what happened?"

"This kid that was the camp tender, he said he was so struck with fear that he didn't know what to do. He tried to run, but the stranger chased him down. He said the stranger had run out of steam and couldn't look at him straight. Then the stranger pulled himself together and told the kid that if he didn't leave the country and never come back, he would have him hunted down and killed. So the kid took off across country, traveling by night and hiding by day, and that's how he came by Alex's place. He was tired, hungry, and scared for his life."

"And did he say what the stranger looked like?"

Verona flattened her lips together again and said, "Yes, he did."

"Can you tell us what he said?"

She held her gray eyes on Dunbar. "Yes. He said the man was tall, well-dressed, and had light-colored hair."

"And what did you think of that?"

"It reminded me of someone. After the kid had something to eat and took off—it bein' dark then—Alex told me it reminded him of the same man."

"And what next?"

"A week or so later, Alex told me that this man we were reminded of started acting fishy, as if he knew the kid had stopped by and spilled his guts. Time went by, and when this man was gone for the winter, Alex turned up dead."

I caught a glimpse of Dick Ainsworth. He was looking at Borden Crowley as if he had just learned something about him, but I did not detect any expression of disapproval.

Dunbar spoke again. "Could you tell us who it was that Alex Garrison said was acting suspicious? Did he say his name?"

"Yes. It was that man there. Mr. Crowley."

A murmur louder than before ran through the crowd. Borden Crowley raised his hand in a gesture to ask for silence.

"I find this offensive. Very unfair. This is nothing more than hearsay."

Dunbar held him with his eyes. "Perhaps you'd like to hear it from the kid himself." He nodded to Mrs. Deville. She withdrew from Verona's side and headed for the hotel.

Crowley raised his voice. "Oh, this is nonsense! There isn't any such kid. This is all someone's dream."

Dunbar remained calm. "The story does not sound made up. I believe there's an old crime on record, an unsolved murder of a sheepherder up on Old Woman Creek, at about that time."

"Bah. Even if it happened, I wasn't there. Who's to say I was?"

"The kid." Dunbar's eyes flickered to take in Ainsworth and Larose, then passed over Lou and me.

Crowley startled me by pointing straight at me. His voice exploded as he said, "It sure as hell isn't this kid here. The kid in her story would have to be thirty years old now."

"Pretty close," said Dunbar. He turned and waved, and Mrs. Deville stepped forward from the overhang in front of the hotel. At her side walked the thin, nervous man I had seen earlier. The gathered crowd made way for them and then moved closer to those of us in front. Verona moved back a couple of steps as she stared at the newcomer.

Mrs. Deville brought the man to stand next to Dunbar. Crowley's eyes had narrowed, and Ainsworth was studying the newcomer.

Dunbar said "Can you tell us your name?"

The thin man blubbered, as if he was having a hard time making himself speak.

Dunbar patted him on the shoulder. "Calm down. No one's

193

going to do anything to you. We'll try again. Can you tell us your name?"

The man wet his lips, swallowed, coughed, and said, "Jimmy Delf."

The crowd was quiet. The air had begun to cool as the sun slipped in the west, and I felt a chill.

"Enough of this," said Crowley. With Ainsworth at his side, he stepped forward and gave a hard look at Mrs. Deville. "Why are you doing this?" he asked. "Why are you taking up with this old bulldog"—he pointed with his elbow at Verona—"and this puling ship rat?" He motioned with his chin at Jimmy Delf.

Mrs. Deville flinched and made a frown. She said, "I don't participate in this kind of conversation."

Boots Larose pushed forward, between Crowley and Ainsworth, and said, "Well, aren't you a puss?"

I thought, this was it. They were trying to throw Dunbar off track, and if possible set him up. It was as if they were trying again what they couldn't pull together that day on roundup.

I felt a wave of dread as Larose stepped closer and grabbed Mrs. Deville's wrist.

She pulled away, and Dunbar's voice was curt.

"Don't touch her."

Ainsworth and Crowley each stepped aside. Larose squared off, planting his tall dark boots and dangling his hand near the yellow handle of his revolver.

"Ah," he said. "I already did. So what are you going to do?"

"Don't push me."

Larose stretched his nostrils as he gave a small wave of his gun hand. "I didn't think you had it in you."

Quick as a cat, Dunbar moved forward and grabbed Larose by the front of his shirt. He lifted Larose so that only the toes of the long boots touched the ground, and he slapped him back and forth on the face. In another instant, he grabbed the shirt with his other hand as well, jerked Larose off his feet and into a sideways position, and slammed him to the ground.

Larose pushed himself to his feet. Rubbing his chin, he said, "That's the last time you'll ever do that." He made as if he was going to turn away, but he whipped back around with his pistol in his hand. As he was cocking the hammer, Dunbar had his own gun out and fired.

Commotion burst out in the corral behind as the steers spooked. Larose pressed his hand to the spot where his ribs and chest met. Blood appeared between his fingers as he backed up one, two, three steps and fell against the corral planks.

The crowd scattered. Dunbar had Ainsworth and Crowley covered with his pistol. Ainsworth carried a gun, but Crowley, as usual, did not. "Let's finish our conversation," Dunbar said.

Jimmy Delf had run for cover in the direction of the hotel, but Mrs. Deville and I followed him and persuaded him to come back. We marched him toward Dunbar, passing Otto and Carl and the proprietor of the mercantile whose name at the moment I could not remember. Lou Foster was standing by as we came up to the spot where Dunbar was faced off against Ainsworth and Crowley.

Dunbar put his gun in his holster. "Tell us your name again."

The thin man's voice was shaky as he said, "Jimmy Delf."

"Very good. Now, Jimmy, can you tell us if you've ever seen this man before?"

Jimmy stammered with a series of *buh, buh, buh* until he came out with, "Yes."

"Can you tell us where?"

"On Old Woman Creek. About fifteen years ago." Jimmy wet his lips and made the *buh-buh-buh* sound again. He took in a short breath and said, "He-uh-killed my partner, Lunn Woodfill."

A rumble of voices traveled through the crowd, which had

drawn closer to listen.

Crowley glared at Jimmy Delf. "That's a lie."

"It's, it's the truth."

The crowd held its collective breath.

Dick Ainsworth stepped forward, hand near his gun, and said, "Did you call this man a liar?"

Dunbar said, "Yes, he did. And I stand behind it."

Ainsworth squared around. "What do you have to do with any of this, anyway?" He bored at Dunbar with his dark blue eyes.

"We could ask the same of you, but I doubt you'd tell us the answer."

Ainsworth's face hardened. "What's that supposed to mean?"

"I'm guessing that you didn't know why Borden Crowley had you do in Alex Garrison. But he hired you to do it, and you did what you were paid to do."

"Oh, you're out of your mind."

"He was afraid Alex Garrison was onto him, and he was right. But he didn't have the nerve to kill another man himself, so he found someone who didn't have any scruples."

"You don't make any more sense than this old bag here."

Verona's small, gray agate eyes peered out from her cloudy face.

Ainsworth was better than I had given him credit for. While everyone's attention was turned on Dunbar and Verona, Ainsworth drew his gun as he stepped to the side to get a clear shot at Jimmy Delf.

Dunbar whirled and lunged. He raised his hand in the shape of a fin and brought it down like a cleaver on Ainsworth's wrist. The gun fired, and a spurt of sand jumped up a yard away from me. Ainsworth dropped the pistol but brought around his left fist to hit Dunbar. The punch bounced off of Dunbar's shoulder, and the two of them grappled to see which one could lock the other in his arms.

Ainsworth fought like a badger, vicious and relentless. He punched and gouged and kicked, and I believe he would have bitten an ear or a finger if he could. Dunbar fought for control rather than to do damage. After the two of them hit the ground once and came back to their feet, Dunbar settled his grip around Ainsworth's midsection. He raised the man higher than he had lifted Larose, gave a hoist with his hip, and flung the man to the ground. This time, he followed the body, put a knee in the back of Ainsworth's armpit, and held his arm for leverage.

"Now you can make your choice," said Dunbar. "You can hold still, or you can have your arm popped out of joint."

Ainsworth was breathing hard, raising tiny clouds of dust. "Go to hell," he said.

Dunbar pushed with his knee, and the man flattened. "I would say the same to you, but you're not going anywhere. And I'll let these people know why. Crowley hired you to kill Alex Garrison because he didn't have the nerve to do it himself. The only hitch was that Bill Pearson saw you in the neighborhood. So you went away. When Crowley thought enough time had passed, he brought you back. But Bill Pearson recognized you, so you had to do him in. Then when other people seemed to know too much, you silenced them as well. George Hodel the traveling drunk and Mary Weldon the innkeeper." Dunbar applied a little more weight with his knee, then turned his head and said, "Bard, pick up his gun and hang onto it. And now that I think of it, get the other one as well."

I took a couple of steps, leaned over, and picked up Ainsworth's pistol. As I rose to locate Boots Larose's body, which had been lying in the background, I saw Borden Crowley taking uncertain steps toward Dunbar and Ainsworth. He held Larose's yellow-handled revolver with both hands.

I heard myself say, "Hold it right there. Drop it." I had him covered with Ainsworth's pistol.

Crowley dropped the gun.

Dunbar had been distracted enough, however, that Ainsworth was able to twist and buck free. He rolled to one side and reached for the revolver that Crowley had dropped. Dunbar rose up and stepped on Ainsworth's hand but could not stop him from grasping the pistol. Dunbar stepped on the man's wrist, then bent over and pulled at the wrist with both hands. Ainsworth squeezed off a shot that buried a bullet with a *spang!* into a corral plank.

Ainsworth rose to his knees, both hands on the pistol, as Dunbar continued to try to control the wrist of the hand that held the gun. Ainsworth rose halfway to his feet, and Dunbar twisted the wrist. The shorter man turned, and the two of them hit the ground again. A gunshot fired, muffled, sounding something like a shot fired down into a prairie dog hole.

Dunbar rolled over and pushed himself onto his knees. Ainsworth lolled on his back, and a wet stain showed on his dark blue shirt.

Dunbar stood up. I still held Crowley at gunpoint, though I do not know what I would have done if he had challenged me.

"And now you," said Dunbar.

Crowley had a strange expression about him, darkened by the gathering dusk. On one hand, he seemed to recognize not only that his jig was up but that someone had come for him. On the other, he seemed to hold on to the attitude that people below him had no right to bring him to account.

To Dunbar he said, "You can't do things like this and get away with it."

Dunbar frowned. "Let's not get off track. You still haven't answered to what happened on Old Woman Creek, not to mention what happened later."

"Nothing happened. It's all a lie." With contempt on his face,

Crowley turned to Jimmy Delf. "I don't know what this guttersnipe hopes to gain by it."

I was struck with the realization that Crowley *was* answering to what happened on Old Woman Creek, even if he was lying.

Dunbar held his eyes on Crowley, who averted his. Dunbar said, "You know he's telling the truth. Your old secret is out. This is your reckoning."

Crowley's eyes widened, and as he looked around, I could feel the eyes of the townspeople, the cowhands, and the other ranch owners all fixed on this center of the stage. Crowley's eyes moved over the crowd again, and though he seemed immobilized, somewhere in his mind, a cog or wheel moved. With the town looking on, he broke and ran.

CHAPTER FOURTEEN

It made no sense. Here was a man at his last ditch with nowhere to go. The end was inevitable. And yet he ran.

He turned and dashed for the main gate of the corrals. Throwing the wooden latch, he ran into the alleyway and left the gate open. Half the crowd saw him as he ran to a saddled horse that was tied by a neck rope. I thought he would try to get away on the horse, but he held his hand against the front of its chest as he looked on both sides. It occurred to me that he was looking for a rifle. Not finding one, he untied the catch rope from the side of the saddle and hurried on with the coiled rope in his hand.

With Dunbar in pursuit, he ran to the cross alley, opened and latched the gates, and ran further into the maze. I thought, he had to know he was doomed. How much time did he think he could buy? Even if he could overcome Dunbar, which I doubted, or escape him and leave the corrals behind, where was he going to run? He would be a man alone, on foot, in the middle of a thousand miles of grassland.

Yet he ran. From time to time I saw his silver-gray hat bobbing above the corral planks, which no longer shone in the sunlight. Not far behind, I saw Dunbar's black hat marking his progress. The chase had an unreal or fantastic quality to it as the two men, the dull corral planks, and the shifting forms of cattle became less distinct with the onset of dusk.

I do not think anyone left the crowd. Mrs. Deville and Verona and Jimmy Delf stood together, as did the small groups of townsfolk and workmen. Carl Granger had climbed up the outer corral planks to gain a better view, and Otto Trent stood on the ground nearby.

Now the light-colored hat came into clearer view. Crowley was climbing the steps of the catwalk.

I thought, how foolish could he be? He was going to a more difficult place to escape from—an easier place to be trapped and not be able to string out his time any longer. Then it occurred to me that he was looking over the layout, planning an escape—again, a pointless escape, for even if he made it to a gate in the rear, he would have no place to go. All he would find would be a set of train tracks and an empty landscape.

Dunbar clattered up the steps behind him. Crowley moved at a fast walk. Dunbar ran. Crowley stopped and turned, then slapped at his pursuer with the coils of the rope.

I knew it hurt. I had slapped at massive, muscle-bound, immovable bulls with a rope like that, and the bull would flinch.

Dunbar put up his hand, caught hold of the rope, and pulled it away from Crowley. The tall man grabbed at the rope to try to take it back, but Dunbar yanked it and kept possession. Crowley turned and ran again.

Dunbar's bootheels sounded on the planks as he took up the chase. He had the coils in his left hand and was swinging the rope with his right.

He's going to catch him, I thought. *He'll bring him back alive.*

Crowley reached the end of the catwalk. He must have planned his route, for he began to climb over the railing. Someone like Boots Larose would have vaulted over the edge and dropped the eight or nine feet to the ground below, but Crowley was not young and supple. He raised his leg, saw that he could not swing his leg over the railing, and repositioned himself.

Dunbar made his toss from fifteen feet away as Crowley swung his leg over and straddled the railing. The loop settled over his shoulders. Holding onto the board with his left hand, he worked his right thumb under the rope and pushed it up over his shoulder. As he did so, his hat fell away.

Dunbar was pulling slack and setting his heels. Crowley tottered as he tried to lift the rope higher. Dunbar shook out slack, the way a cowpuncher does to settle the rope over a calf's nose and onto its neck, except that Dunbar was trying to drop the rope back down around Crowley's upper arms. The loss of tension on the rope caused Crowley to totter again. The catwalk was high enough, and the rail even higher, that I was able to see him hover and slip.

His right leg pointed straight down, resting on nothing, and his left leg kicked for a plank to grab onto. There was no plank, just the railing. He tried to hook his leg on that lone two-by-four, but his balance was too far off.

Dunbar must have thought he had the rope lower, for he pulled the slack and leaned back as Crowley tumbled over. The rope tightened around his neck, and his fall stopped just before his feet could touch the ground.

Years later, I would come upon a man who had hanged himself from a trestle. When I did, I recalled this image that stayed with me of a man suspended for a few seconds in the dusk until he tumbled on the ground.

Del Bancroft came to visit us at the chuck wagon the next morning. Dan and the night wrangler had set camp in the same spot as when we were building the corrals, and Dunbar and I had pitched our tent as before. Some of the other cowhands had camped out as well, including George and Bob, while others had taken rooms or gone back to their ranches. Only a couple of other hands were stirring when Del poured a cup of coffee and sat down next to Dunbar and me.

Other than the background noise of livestock grunting and bumping in the corrals, the predawn morning at the edge of town was still and quiet. Del had a fresh air about him, with the scent of bath soap, and I saw the neat, clean edges where he had trimmed around his beard.

"We'll be goin' home in a little while," he said. "Don't know when I'll see you again."

Dunbar said, "I expect to pull out in a day or two."

"I'll be around," I said.

"We're planning to go to Lincoln. Be gone about two weeks."

Dunbar and I nodded.

After a sip of coffee, Del directed his attention to Dunbar. "Thinkin' I might not see you again, I thought I might ask you a question."

"Go ahead."

"How did you know about Jimmy Delf?"

Dunbar raised his eyebrows and drew in a breath. "Well, I had been following this case for a while, along with a few others. Gathering information as I could. I was able to track him down where he was living in town called Corinth in Illinois. After I spoke with him, I thought his story was believable, so I came here to put things together."

"To find out the truth. Well, I'm glad you did. You must be some kind of an investigator, then. Maybe a Pinkerton man?"

"I work on my own."

Del nodded as he registered the information. "It's too bad about Crowley."

"In what way?" Dunbar had an open expression on his face, as if the comment were a point of philosophical interest.

"I would like to have seen him brought before a court of law. And I assume that's what you were attempting."

"It was."

Del gave a mild shrug. "There's no way of changing it. As for Larose, there was no way around how that ended."

"Not that I could see."

Del paused and gazed at the fire. "I don't know what to make of him. He wasn't in on it from the beginning, that's for sure. It goes too far back."

"True. I think he came into the game late and didn't realize what he was getting into. I think he was trying to prove himself so he could move up and have a position above the others. Still, he bought into the game and took cards. Pulling a gun on another man is serious business, so my guess is that he helped Ainsworth with the two jobs in town. He had something to protect."

"That makes sense. I had known him for a while, and I was surprised to see how thick he was becoming with Ainsworth. Now him, I never much cared for. But he was someone else's hired man, so I tried not to pay him much attention. As for Crowley, that just goes to show that you can know someone for years and not know at all what's at the bottom. Lookin' back, I can't say I ever knew him. He had skeletons in the closet all that time."

Del's wording reminded me of something Dunbar had said one day after we had stopped by Blue Wolf Spring. Hidden bodies, or secret crimes, were like people who fell into glaciers—always there.

Dunbar pursed his lips, and his mustache bushed up. "Like they say in the old poems, 'murder will out.' You'd like to think it's a dependable truth, but it doesn't happen as often as it should. Too many people still get away with it."

"Well, he didn't."

"You can see now that it weighed on him. Even after having Alex Garrison killed, he had the shack burned down. My guess is that he was afraid there might be some kind of a written statement tucked away. Then he felt that Bill Pearson posed too much of a threat. After that, killing George Hodel was unnecessary, but the man had come down from the north, and from all his comments about where he had been and what he'd seen, Crowley must have thought he had heard something about the incident on Old Woman Creek. It made Crowley desperate."

Del stared at the fire for a few seconds, as if he was putting things together. "I said I had a question, and you've answered two at least. I hope you don't mind if I ask a third."

"No harm."

"What about Mrs. Deville? How does she happen to take part in this?"

"She offered to help."

"Is she some kind of a detective?"

"No, she's been in the restaurant business, as she said."

"But you are."

"I'm a cowpuncher."

Del smiled. "I knew that." He turned to me. "Tag, I was wondering if you could look after our place while we're gone."

"I suppose I could. I think my work is just about up with Lou Foster."

"Good. We'll be leaving in three days. If you can come by on Thursday, I'll show you what to do."

He stood up, and I did likewise. We shook hands.

Dunbar stood up as well. As he shook hands with Del Bancroft, he said, "Have a safe trip. It's been good to work with you."

"Yes, it has. If you ever come back through, drop by and see us."

"I might. I'd like to see that stagecoach when you've got it turned out."

Jimmy Delf left the same day. He stopped by to see us while we were pitching hay to the cattle in the pens.

"I'm leaving on the train in a little while," he said. He still looked worried, but his face was not as ghostly as before.

"The eastbound?" I asked.

"Uh-huh." His eyes shifted to Dunbar. "I want to thank you for what you did. This thing has been hangin' over me for fifteen years. I've always been lookin' over my shoulder to see if someone caught up with me. Runnin' off and leavin' Lunn like I did, I never felt right. I can't help thinkin' he'll rest easier in his grave now."

"I hope so," said Dunbar.

"You made the son of a bitch pay for what he did."

"It wasn't my intention to do it all myself, but what's done is done."

"Well, I'll remember you for it." He put out his hand, which still had a tremble. He shook with Dunbar and then with me.

I said, "So long, Jimmy. Thanks for coming here."

"I had to. I was scared to death, but I had to."

Dunbar said, "You did well, Jimmy. Good luck to you."

Jimmy turned and walked away, a thin and lonely and not very powerful man, but a person who had ventured to tell the truth when the time came. I imagined he was not going back to a very prosperous life, but at least he would not have to look over his shoulder all the time.

I thought Mrs. Deville would leave on the same train as Jimmy Delf, but she didn't. To my surprise, she left on the westbound train the next day at noon. Dunbar and I had stayed over to help load the steers into the stock cars. George and Bob and one of the men from Hat Creek were going to ride in the caboose to Omaha. At every stop they would have to go along the cars with poles and roust the animals to their feet. I had heard it was a mucky job, but these three fellows were cheerful about the prospect. The eastbound stock train would not roll in until later in the afternoon, but the boys already had their bags packed at midday and had bought cigars. They sat around camp, idle and fidgeting.

When the whistle of the westbound sounded a couple of miles out, Dunbar left the camp and crossed the street toward the hotel. A couple of minutes later, he emerged with Mrs. Deville at his side. She was dressed as she had been the first time I saw her, in a dark traveling hat, a gray linen duster, and gray gloves. Dunbar carried her brown Gladstone bag.

The train chugged and hissed to a stop. A porter jumped down from the second passenger car and placed a step on the ground. Dunbar handed the lady up into the car, where she turned on the first step and paused to smile at him. He took off his dark hat and swept it in front of him as he bowed. Mrs. Deville's teeth showed in a larger smile, and she disappeared from my sight. Dunbar stood by, hat at his side, as the porter took the bag and set it, along with the portable step, in the entry to the passenger car. He pulled himself up and in as the train began to move. A minute later, the train let out a whistle as it picked up steam and rolled away to the west.

Dunbar and I returned to the ranch late that afternoon, after we had loaded the steers. I thought he would at least spend the night, but he had a purposeful air about him as he packed his few things in the bunkhouse and fitted out the buckskin packhorse. As he worked, I heard him whistling the tune of the song about the woman who died in the snow.

He had left the blue roan saddled, so he was ready to go in a short while. He led the two horses into the yard and stopped. He had not yet put on his gloves after the detailed work of buckling straps and tying knots, and I saw the dark spot in his palm when he reached forward to shake.

"My best to you, Bard. I wish you good luck."

"And the same to you. I thought you might stay longer."

"It's a good thought, but I've got things to do."

"Well, we've had a good time, when we weren't having to deal with these undesirable things. I enjoyed our conversations."

"So did I. Always a good time."

I looked at the ground, then up at him. "I don't want to sound like I'm echoing Del Bancroft, but I have a question."

He laughed. "Does that mean three?"

"I think just one. And I hope you don't mind. It's about Mrs. Deville."

He smiled. "I'm sure you wouldn't ask anything ungallant. Go ahead."

"I had the impression that you knew her from before."

"I never said I didn't."

"Then why do you leave her, or let her leave you? She's such a beautiful woman."

"Ah, that's a young man's question. Not that I'm old, in years at least. But I'll answer it. Like I've said, I've got work to do. And it's getting later in the year."

"Do you think you'll see her again?"

"There's nothing that says I can't. No fate or prophecy that I'm aware of. And that's three questions, after all."

To me, it was one question that had three parts, but I took his comment in good humor. "Very well," I said. "Thank you for all you've done. If Lunn Woodfill can sleep easier in his grave, maybe Alex Garrison can, too." I felt that he had kept his word with Mrs. Pearson, but I could not bring myself to mention Bill Pearson, George Hodel, or Mary Weldon, for in truth, I did not think enough justice had been served, though there was nothing more to be done.

He must have had a similar thought. "I wish I could have done more," he said.

We shook again, and he moved his horses into position. Holding the lead rope out of the way, he pulled himself into the saddle with one hand, reined the blue roan around, and moved forward. He raised his dark hat in farewell and said, "So long."

He rode out of the yard and headed north, the two horses stepping along at a brisk pace. Evening was drawing in, and within a few minutes, I could see only hazy shapes. I imagined Mrs. Deville, several hours farther down the railroad line, looking out the window upon a similar darkening landscape. When I focused again in Dunbar's direction, the shapes of him and his horses had been absorbed in the dusk.

I knew that the railroad veered north and northwest when it met the other line coming up from Cheyenne. Moistness came to my eyes as I thought of the sacrifice Dunbar was making, even if it was not permanent. I hoped he and Mrs. Deville would meet again, but then I told myself that it was none of my business, and I made myself think no more about that aspect for the time being.

I never heard of or from Dunbar again, and he never came by to see how Del Bancroft turned out the restored stagecoach. From time to time I can't help wondering whether he met up with Mrs. Deville. On a lesser note, I sometimes wonder if he ever made up a song of his own, as he had said on a day that now seems distant and innocent, though I know he was working even then.

After he left, those of us in the Niobrara country went about our lives. To me it seemed as if our area had been purged of a disease that we had not been much aware of. So we went on to face the continuing facts of our lives—snow and ice in the winter, heat and grasshoppers in the summer, wind at all seasons, death and illness as they came.

Lou Foster made it through the following winter and began

to improve when the warm weather came around again. He recovered enough to get around without a crutch, but he still walks with a limp and uses a step or block to help himself onto a horse. Bob Crenshaw stayed in the East, but George Olney returned the next season and now works year-round at the ranch. He brings the horse around for Lou Foster, and he makes sure the boss does not step on ice.

Dan the cook, meanwhile, still works at the ranch, though his steps are slower now. He still waters the elm tree outside the bunkhouse. It has grown tall and bushy, and Dan sits in its shade on summer afternoons.

Verona still works for Luke Hayward, though I hear that she does not get around very well at all. When I think of her, I remember the courage she had to stand up to Borden Crowley, and I hope she is living out her days in peace as she leans on her stick amidst the pens of animals and the strange call of the peacock.

Fred Mullet went on to work for the Converse Cattle Company and the 77 Ranch, and he has become well known for the stories he tells about ancient crimes on Old Woman Creek and south of the Hat Creek Breaks. The last time I saw him, he was starting to show gray around the temples. He spoke of cowpunching as if it were a curse, and he said that as soon as the 77 could do without him, he was going to find a woman and settle down.

The Bower remained closed for a couple of years until Matthew Fenster, the proprietor of the mercantile, bought the building and rented it out to a man who runs a saddle shop and does hat repair.

The BC ranch passed into the hands of an investment company, which tried to run it as a ranch from a distance but ended up selling it off in the separate deeded parts that Borden Crowley had amassed.

With the help of Del Bancroft, I bought the parcel that had belonged to Alex Garrison. Emma and I have built a cabin there, and we have planted a few trees. We water them with good clear water from Blue Wolf Spring, here in the midst of a vast and often dry garden of grass.

ABOUT THE AUTHOR

John D. Nesbitt lives in the plains country of Wyoming, where he teaches English and Spanish at Eastern Wyoming College. He writes western, contemporary, mystery, and retro/noir fiction as well as nonfiction and poetry. John has won many awards for his work, including two awards from the Wyoming State Historical Society (for fiction), two awards from Wyoming Writers for encouragement of other writers and service to the organization, two Wyoming Arts Council literary fellowships (one for fiction, one for nonfiction), two Will Rogers Medallion Awards (one for western poetry, one for fiction), and three Spur awards from Western Writers of America. His most recent books are *Death in Cantera* and *Destiny at Dry Camp*, frontier mysteries with Five Star.

The employees of Five Star Publishing hope you have enjoyed this book.

Our Five Star novels explore little-known chapters from America's history, stories told from unique perspectives that will entertain a broad range of readers.

Other Five Star books are available at your local library, bookstore, all major book distributors, and directly from Five Star/Gale.

Connect with Five Star Publishing

Visit us on Facebook:
  https://www.facebook.com/FiveStarCengage

Email:
  FiveStar@cengage.com

For information about titles and placing orders:
  (800) 223-1244
  gale.orders@cengage.com

To share your comments, write to us:
  Five Star Publishing
  Attn: Publisher
  10 Water St., Suite 310
  Waterville, ME 04901